The Danger Within

Valerie Hansen

Steeple
Hill®

Published by Steeple Hill Books™

To Joe, who loves me even when he thinks
I'm crazy—which is most of the time!

Special thanks and acknowledgment are given to
Valerie Hansen for her contribution to the
FAITH AT THE CROSSROADS series.

STEEPLE HILL BOOKS

Steeple Hill®

ISBN 0-373-87347-6

THE DANGER WITHIN

www.SteepleHill.com

Printed in U.S.A.

"The barn's on fire!"

Layla rounded the corner and slid to a stop, gasping a heartfelt "Thank You, God!" when she realized there was no immediate danger to animals or buildings.

A pile of soiled hay was doing its best to burn in spite of the frigid temperatures. She didn't want to leave the pile smoldering that close to a vulnerable building so she grabbed a pitchfork and proceeded to scatter the old hay to cool it.

The tines of the pitchfork hit something hard. Layla scraped away the glowing embers to reveal a blackened feed pan. She didn't have to look closely to see the scrape marks she'd left on it when she'd taken her lab samples.

One mystery was resolved. When someone had tried to destroy the evidence, they'd admitted to purposely poisoning Michael Vance's innocent cattle.

* * *

FAITH AT THE CROSSROADS: Can faith and love sustain two families against a diabolical enemy?

Books by Valerie Hansen

Love Inspired

*The Wedding Arbor #84
*The Troublesome Angel #103
*The Perfect Couple #119
*Second Chances #139
*Love One Another #154
*Blessings of the Heart #206
*Samantha's Gift #217
*Everlasting Love #270

*Serenity, Arkansas

Love Inspired Suspense

Her Brother's Keeper #10
The Danger Within #15

VALERIE HANSEN

was thirty when she awoke to the presence of the Lord in her life and turned to Jesus. In the years that followed she worked with young children, both in church and secular environments. She also raised a family of her own and played foster mother to a wide assortment of furred and feathered critters.

Married to her high school sweetheart since age seventeen, she now lives in an old farmhouse she and her husband renovated with their own hands. She loves to hike the wooded hills behind the house and reflect on the marvelous turn her life has taken. Not only is she privileged to reside among the loving, accepting folks in the breathtakingly beautiful Ozark Mountains of Arkansas, she also gets to share her personal faith by telling the stories of her heart for Steeple Hill's Love Inspired line. Life doesn't get much better than that!

Keep me, O Lord, from the hands of the wicked;
preserve me from the violent men; who have
purposed to overthrow my goings.
—*Psalms* 140:4

CAST OF CHARACTERS

Michael Vance—His cows kept getting sick and dying. Were they succumbing to disease or was someone poisoning them?

Layla Dixon—Working as the temporary ranch veterinarian and helping uncover the secrets behind the ailments of the cows kept the bohemian beauty close to Michael.

El Jefe—Who was the man also known as Chief? What did he have to do with the new influx of drugs into Colorado Springs? And why was he so intent on bringing down the Vance and Montgomery families?

Hector Delgato—Michael's secretive new foreman was never around whenever bad things happened....

Prologue

"We have to be careful, *El Jefe*."

"*Now* you think of that? I told you not to trust an amateur like Ritchie Stark with a job as important as taking care of Mayor Vance."

"It's not my fault. Everything would have been fine if Ritchie hadn't brought in one of his flunkies to do the job instead of handling it himself."

"Fine? Hah! The guy botched it. Twice. And that nurse saw him the second time. She can identify him."

"Chloe Tanner? Not necessarily. He hit her pretty hard. We can't be positive how much she remembers."

"All the same, now that she's tied up with that FBI man it's even more dangerous for us. We need to eliminate any witnesses who can lead the Feds back to us."

"Well, don't look at me! I have a reputation to protect."

"Never mind," The Chief, *El Jefe*'s Anglicized code name, rasped angrily. "I'll do it myself, starting with that idiot friend of Ritchie's."

"We mustn't act foolishly. I know you want success as much as I do but we must not call undue attention to this situation. Right now, everyone is concentrating on the mayor's condition, hoping he'll come out of the coma and be able to help the police. If there are more accidents or deaths associated with him, someone may suspect a conspiracy."

The Chief snorted. "If they do, it'll be the first intelligent conclusion they've come to."

"Still…"

"I'll be careful. This time, it'll look like an accident. Like you said, I want this plan to succeed. And you're going to help me."

"My pleasure. The sooner you get what you want and make us both even richer, the happier I'll be."

"There's more at stake here than merely a fortune in drugs. I have a score to settle with the Vance and Montgomery families. Nothing is going to stop me."

"Or me," his companion added.

"Good." His laugh was sinister and guttural. "Because I would give up my life itself, if I knew my enemies would die with me."

Chapter One

Layla Dixon lifted her face to the sun, closed her eyes and stood motionless, basking in the clean, welcoming feel of the high country. Of all the places she'd been, this part of Colorado came the closest to feeling like home. It truly was "God's Country."

She sighed, smiled. It had been a good idea to wander in this direction. After all, it wasn't as if she intended to stick around very long. The minute she was made to feel unwelcome, she was history.

She zipped her down-filled vest as she glanced at the hopeful blue heeler waiting for her to let him out of the cab of her pickup. If Colorado Springs hadn't been on the front range of the Rockies where the climate was warmer, the icy chill of early February would have been unbearable. As it was, her breath clouded around her head and her boots squeaked on the thin sheet of snow that dusted the sidewalk.

She opened the passenger side door and ruffled the dog's mottled gray ears. "You wait in the truck, Smokey. I'll bring you back a snack, okay?"

The sad look she got in return made her chuckle. "That won't work this time, old boy. This is for your own good."

He lunged, trying to lick her face.

Layla ducked and laughed. "I'm not changing my mind. I don't care how many kisses you give me." Hugging the dog's muscular neck she told him, "You're such a good boy. I'm so glad we met when we did. I needed a buddy."

The dog wiggled and panted happily in response. Holding up her hand, palm out, she commanded, "Stay," and backed away, closing the door. The windows were down enough for ventilation and the sun was shining in a cloudless sky. Smokey would probably be more comfortable than she was.

Shivering, Layla lifted her scarf to cover her head and wrapped her arms around herself, bangle bracelets jingling. Good thing she was familiar with this area and knew how to dress. She hadn't given up her trademark flowing skirt and favorite silver jewelry but she had been smart enough to slip on sweatpants under the skirt and switch from moccasins to boots. Image was one thing. Freezing to death for the sake of style was another. If her parents had taught her anything, it was to conform to the dictates of nature and go with the flow instead of complaining.

Michael Vance clomped into the Stagecoach Café and shrugged out of his fleece-lined leather jacket before wending his way to his usual table.

He'd kind of hoped café owner Fiona Montgomery would be busy in the kitchen. No such luck. He could see he was in for an inquisition, starting right now. Bright red hair fluffed, grin in place, she was headed straight for him.

"Michael! What brings you into town?"

He snorted as he laid his black felt Stetson on the empty chair beside him. "What doesn't. It's been one of those weeks."

"Uh-oh. It's only Tuesday."

"Tell me about it."

Fiona slid her ample self into the chair across from him and leaned her elbows on the table. "Sounds like you'd better tell *me*. How are things on the Double V? Any word from your foreman?"

Though it wasn't Michael's habit to confide in the local telegraph-in-a-waitress's uniform, he figured it might be for the best in this case. "No. Ben's still missing. The police suspect he had problems with drugs again but I can't believe it. He'd been clean and sober for years, even before I hired him."

"How's that Hector Delgato guy working out in Ben's place?"

"He's okay, I guess. Kind of quiet and moody but he does his job. I heard he has an eye for the ladies. You'd better watch out." Michael gave Fiona a wink.

"Humph. I can handle myself. I've been married to Joe long enough to get all the practice handling unruly men that I'll ever need."

Michael chuckled. "It wouldn't have been any

better if you'd married a Vance. That's exactly what Aunt Lidia always says about Uncle Max."

"Poor man. I heard he's still in a coma."

"Yeah. I stopped at Vance Memorial before I came here. It's tough to see him like that."

"Lidia seems to be holding up okay, considering. I offered to let her come back and cook for me if she wanted, thought she might need the distraction. But she's spending every spare minute at the hospital, holding Max's hand. That's understandable."

"Yeah." Michael ran his fingers through his hair. "All my troubles put together don't amount to a hill of beans compared to theirs."

"I know you're worried about Ben and Max but I get the impression there's more. What else is wrong?"

"Imelda sprained her ankle."

"Oh, no! Is she okay?"

"Actually, I think she's milking the injury for all it's worth. Norberto's been spending most of his time fussing over her, which means I'm not only short a cook, my best ranch hand is too distracted to think straight. A guy like me could starve to death cooking for himself. You don't happen to know of anyone looking for a job as a housekeeper, do you?"

Fiona snorted. "No. Too bad Dorothy Miller's in Florida for the winter or you could ask her to come out of retirement and come back to work for you." She paused, thoughtful. "Say, if it's a cook you want, how about asking at the Galilee Women's Shelter?

I'm sure Susan Dawson knows someone who could use the job and the self-esteem boost."

"I thought of that. And I may. But I was kind of looking for a stable, motherly type, like Dorothy was." He flashed Fiona a lopsided grin. "What are you doing for the next couple of weeks?"

The restaurant owner gave him a playful whack on the forearm. "Running this place and taking care of my Joe. That keeps me plenty busy, thank you."

Michael shrugged. "Well, it was worth a try. How's Joe doing these days?"

"Pretty well, considering. I'm not going to tell him about your problems because he might try to help out. It wouldn't be good for him."

"I know it wouldn't. I've offered to get somebody to come in and take good care of Imelda to free up Norberto but he won't hear of it. He's like a mother hen around her."

"Love is like that."

Michael made a face. "I wouldn't know."

"You can't count Tammy. She was wrong for you from the get-go. I'm just glad you saw through her before you made the biggest mistake of your life."

"Yeah, right." He cocked his head toward the kitchen. "So, what's the special today? I figure I'd better fill up while I'm here."

Fiona patted his hand as she got to her feet and took out her order pad. "We're featuring the Smoked Salmon Caesar Salad but I know you're strictly a meat-and-potatoes man. How about the Roasted Pork Green Chili? I've got fresh-baked corn bread to go with it."

"Sounds good." He scanned the growing lunch crowd. "Have you seen Doc Pritchard lately? I've been calling his office and all I get is the answering machine."

"That's all you will get for a while. He's having some sort of midlife crisis, I guess. Took off for Vegas and left old Wilt in charge."

Michael grimaced. "That's what I was afraid of."

"Why? What do you need a vet for?"

He lowered his voice and spoke aside. "I've lost five head recently. No sickness, no symptoms of disease. They just keeled over. I'm not about to trust the rest of the herd to Wilt. He retired from practice twenty years ago. His methods of diagnosis have to be outdated."

"You going to bring in another vet then?"

Michael again raked his fingers through his thick, dark hair. "I don't know yet. I hate to. The last thing we ranchers need is to have the government get in a tizzy over nothing and quarantine us before we figure out what's causing the problem. The price of beef is already unsteady."

"Well, no wonder your chin is draggin' the ground. You just sit there and relax for a bit. I'll get your order in and bring you a cup of coffee while you wait. How's that sound?"

"Better than anything that's happened to me lately," Michael said. "And a piece of your famous apple pie, too, please."

"Gladly. Back in a jiffy."

Michael watched Fiona wend her way between the

red-checkered, cloth-covered tables, greeting patrons as she went. The decor of the place was rustic and Western and the food was superb, but the real ambience came from its owner. Fiona radiated a homespun warmth that gave the Stagecoach Café its special aura of welcome, of home. Though her pride in the restaurant's offerings was understandable, he suspected she could have served mundane fast food like any generic burger joint and been just as successful.

Speaking of burgers... Michael's gut twisted. The mysterious losses he'd experienced hadn't looked as though they were caused by any known bovine diseases but anything was possible, even though remote. The Double V was his life. His reason for being. His uncle Max, his sister, Holly, and most of his cousins had gone into some form of law enforcement. That kind of career had never appealed to him. He was man of the land. A rancher to the core. If he lost the ranch...

Philippians 4:6 popped into his mind and made him smile. "Yeah," he said, trying not to be cynical, "'Be anxious for nothing...'" *Easier said than done.* It was almost as hard to trust the Lord and not worry as it was to give thanks for the mess he was in.

Fiona delivered his meal and he bowed quietly over it to whisper, "Thank You for this food, Lord. Please be patient. I'm working on thanking You for the other stuff."

Michael sighed, then added an honestly reverent, "Amen."

* * *

Layla hesitated at the door of the busy restaurant. The red, barnlike building had been an empty, run-down relic of the nineteenth century the last time she'd visited Colorado Springs. Whoever had renovated it had done a monumental job of restoration. Curiosity urged her to open the door. Once she did, tantalizing aromas drew her inside without a second thought. She might not choose to eat meat but that didn't mean she couldn't appreciate well-prepared cuisine.

She slipped off her scarf, propped one hip on the nearest stool and leaned an elbow on the small counter just inside the entrance. A woman with hair the color of a shiny fire truck hurried over.

"Afternoon. Something to drink?" Fiona asked.

"No, thanks. I'm just waiting for a table. I can eat out here if you're too full."

"Nonsense. We'll find you a place in a jiffy. What brings you to Colorado Springs?"

"Just passing through," Layla said pleasantly. "I used to live around here, years ago."

"Really?" There was no condemnation in the titian-haired woman's expression when she said, "Maybe I knew you. I used to have lots of friends from the hippie commune on the way to Cripple Creek."

"Then you may have heard of my family. I'm Layla Rainbow Dixon. My mother is Carol and my dad's Gilbert."

"Dixon? Not Carol 'Moonsong' and Gilbert 'River' Dixon!"

"That's them."

"Well, well, what a small world. What're they up to these days? Still selling organic vegetables?"

"Actually, they run an herb business on the Internet. Dad may be sold on the simple life but it hasn't stopped him from taking advantage of modern conveniences."

"You don't say. How about the little ones? Didn't you have a brother and sister?"

"Sure did. My brother Hendrix is a stockbroker. My sister designs clothes." Layla lifted a side panel of her flowing skirt and held it out in a soft drape. "Petal's specialty is wedding couture but she designed this to look like a rainbow, just for me. I love it, don't you?"

"It's beautiful with your blond hair and blue eyes." Fiona patted her bright coif. "Afraid it would clash with my *natural* coloring, though."

Trying to keep from looking incredulous, Layla smiled. "It sure might." She scanned the busy room. "So, do you work here or is this your place?"

"It's all mine. Mine and the bank's," Fiona quipped. "What do you do, travel around and sell your sister's designs?"

"No, no." Layla's soft curls danced as she shook her head. "I may not look like it, but I have a degree in veterinary medicine." Seeing the older woman's jaw drop she frowned. "What? Did I say something wrong?"

"No, no. Where do you practice?"

"Here and there. I'm not tied down to an office,

if that's what you mean. I like the freedom of going where I want, when I want."

Fiona glanced over her shoulder. "Tell you what. It could be half an hour or more before a table opens up. Would you mind if I sat you with another customer?"

Layla shrugged. "I guess not. I am pretty hungry."

"Terrific." She whirled and started away at a fast pace. "Follow me. I think I have the perfect place for you."

Michael was deep in thought and concentrating on his bowl of chili and corn bread when Fiona approached. He looked up expecting her to offer a coffee refill. Instead, he saw her pointing to the opposite side of his small table. Beside her stood a blonde who looked like a cross between a country music wannabe and a gypsy. *Mostly gypsy,* he decided after a more careful perusal that included the multiple earrings peeking through her loose curls. She could have been a flower child of the sixties, except she was far too young.

Fiona was beaming. "Michael, honey, we're out of room. Do you mind sharing?"

Before he could answer she prattled on. "I think the Lord has already answered our prayers. I'd like you to meet Layla Dixon. That's *Doctor* Dixon. She's a vet. Isn't that wonderful? She was just passing through and look where she decided to stop for lunch."

Michael pushed back his chair and stood politely, napkin in hand. The young woman looked amiable enough but he was far from pleased by Fiona's well-intentioned interference.

"Michael Vance. Pleased to meet you." He briefly shook the hand Layla offered and was startled at how cold—and how soft—her fingers were. "You're freezing," he said. "Here. Sit down and grab a cup of hot coffee."

"I don't drink coffee," she said pleasantly. "I would like a cup of tea, though."

"Fine." He looked to Fiona. "And bring her some of this chili. It's hot enough to melt an iceberg."

"No, really, I..." Layla scowled.

"Sorry. I didn't mean to be pushy. Everything here is good. Have whatever you like."

"Thanks, I will." Smiling, Layla swept her skirt gracefully aside and slid into the chair opposite him before unzipping her vest. "Please, continue eating. I didn't mean to interrupt your meal." She looked up at Fiona. "I'll have herb tea and a Chef's salad with only eggs and cheese. I don't eat meat. Ranch dressing, please."

Michael's eyebrows rose at Layla's choices as Fiona went to place the order. "Rabbit food?"

"It's good for rabbits, isn't it?"

"They tend to be pretty puny."

"Only because that's the way the Lord intended them to be. I'd hate to see a bunny the size of a horse." One eyebrow arched. "Come to think of it, horses are vegetarians, too."

"I can see you're an expert," Michael quipped. "Did they teach you that in veterinary college?"

"Nope. I already knew. I'm not a city girl. I was raised not far from here."

"Really? Let me guess, around Manitou Springs?"

"Yes, as a matter of fact. How did you know?"

Michael saw her glance at her bangle bracelets, then start to finger the beads in one of the necklaces draped in silvery loops around her neck. She knew very well how he'd come to that conclusion and was obviously waiting for him to make some derogatory comment about life in a commune.

Instead, he nodded toward the chair where he'd placed his hat. "The same way you know I'm a rancher. We both dress the part."

"I do have my conventional side."

"You must, to have graduated as a veterinarian. Where did you go to school?"

"Up by Berkeley. The UC Davis campus." Layla began to grin. "That way I didn't have to buy a new wardrobe."

"Very practical." Michael paused as her tea and salad were delivered. "What brings you back to Colorado?"

Holding the cup in both hands to warm her fingers, she took a cautious sip. "Umm. I don't know, exactly. I travel a lot. Here and there."

"That's it?" Michael was incredulous. "You just drift?"

"I like to see new sights. It suits my nature."

He swallowed his last spoonful of lunch and settled back in his chair. "Amazing. I can't imagine ever wanting to do that. This place is home."

Layla smiled indulgently. "Any place can be home if your heart is right and you're in tune with the Lord."

"Sounds like you've kept the earthy philosophy you grew up with and substituted God for Mother Nature."

"I didn't need to substitute anything. It all belongs to God in the first place."

"Good point."

She nodded slowly. "I seem to remember a verse about Him owning the cattle on a thousand hills."

"I've heard it. I just wish He was watching the livestock at my place a little closer."

"Why?"

Michael shook his head soberly. "Never mind. It's nothing. I'll get it all sorted out soon."

"Maybe I can help. I'd be glad to give you a professional opinion if you want."

In spite of her age and nonconformist image he was tempted to take her up on the offer. However, once he confided in her there'd be no going back. Although she seemed friendly and concerned, it was foolish to expect loyalty—or silence—from someone he hardly knew.

"Thanks. I can handle it myself."

"Good for you," she said with a quirky smile. Her gaze settled on the table next to his empty chili bowl. "Are you going to eat those crackers?"

"No. Help yourself. I would have offered if they'd been whole wheat."

"I have been known to consume refined flour on

occasion. I make up for it by eating right the rest of the time. You know. Nuts, berries, twigs, whatever."

"Glad to hear it." He crumpled his napkin and placed it beside his empty bowl. "Well, it's been nice meeting you. If you'll excuse me…"

"Thanks for sharing your table—and your crackers."

"You're quite welcome. Have a nice life— wherever you decide to go."

"Thanks. I will."

Michael picked up his hat and squared it on his head. He was turning away when the phone in his pocket jingled. He flipped it open and answered. "Hello?"

"We got a problem, boss."

Listening to Norberto explain what he meant by that, Michael scowled. "Have you done all you can?"

"*Sí*, boss."

"What about Hector? Where's he?"

"Gone. He didn't say where."

"Terrific. Okay. I'm on my way."

"Trouble?" Layla asked as Michael ended the telephone conversation.

"Yeah." He studied her for a long moment. "What do you know about cows? Calving, to be more precise."

"I paid attention in class, if that's what you're asking. Why?"

"We've got a special heifer in labor. Norberto, my best hand, says nobody can get close enough to check her. He thinks the calf is breech."

Suddenly all business, Layla put down her fork and stood to face him. "How long has she been in labor? Is she out on the range or inside? Has he checked for the calf's tail? Is the heifer down yet? Have her hips gone out?"

Michael held up his hand. "Whoa. We've got her in the barn but the rest I don't know. Normally, we'd just let her go ahead and try until she got too tired and sore to fight us, then we'd step in and help. But this heifer is a 4-H project I bought at the fair last year. She belonged to one of the little girls from church. I promised I'd take extra good care of her."

"Then we'd better get a move on. How far is your ranch?" As she spoke, she was scooping up the cellophane-wrapped crackers and stuffing them into her pockets.

"You don't have to do this."

"Of course I do! It's what I went to school for. Besides, I have a way with animals."

"It might help to have a woman there," Michael reasoned. "I imagine the heifer remembers her first owner. Okay. You're hired. But just for today. Just till we get the calf on the ground."

He threw enough money on the table to pay for both their lunches and followed Layla. She was already almost to the door and practically running. If her skill matched her enthusiasm, maybe he hadn't made such an arbitrary decision after all. And, maybe Fiona was right. Maybe the offbeat vet had been brought to Colorado Springs at that particular time because the Lord knew she'd be needed. Stranger things had happened in Michael's life, especially lately.

He grabbed his jacket and shrugged into it as he shouldered out the door after Layla.

Chapter Two

"My truck's parked a little way down the block," Layla said. "What're you driving? I'll follow you."

"This black dually. See the Double V logo on the door?" He pointed. "What color's your truck?"

Layla's smile was crooked, her blue eyes twinkling. "Kind of purple," she said, "with artistic splotches of pink and green. Picture a camo paint job in pastels."

"I can hardly wait."

She gave him a cynical look. "Listen, mister. I'm not griping about your boring black truck so I suggest you keep your opinions of my color choices to yourself."

"Yes, ma'am." He touched the brim of his hat respectfully and nodded.

Layla was pleased to see the corners of his mouth twitch as if he were suppressing a smile. The man might dress like an ad for an upscale farm store and wear a black hat, but if he was this worried about a little girl's pet cow he definitely had the heart of someone who deserved the white hat of a Western hero. That was good enough for her.

Pulling on his gloves Michael warned, "Watch your speed. These roads can be treacherous, especially in bad weather. Do you have four-wheel drive?"

"No, but my truck does." She chuckled softly, waiting for him to catch on and laugh. He ignored the joke.

"Good. Use it when we turn off highway 24 onto 67. That road can be pretty tricky if you aren't familiar with it."

"I've driven up there before. I'll be fine."

"Okay. In case we get separated, my spread is the Double V. There's a sign at the main entrance."

"Got it." Layla started away, calling over her shoulder, "Don't worry. You won't be able to lose me if you try."

Lose her? Michael was already having enough second thoughts that that didn't sound like a bad idea.

His conscience immediately reared and kicked like a wild mustang on a short halter rope. It went against his nature to make a promise he didn't intend to keep. Besides, the kooky woman probably could help. Once the calf was delivered, however, he was going to send this unconventional lady packing. He had enough problems without adding someone like her into the mix.

Michael circled his truck, climbed behind the wheel and started the engine. Clouds of exhaust formed in the crisp mountain air, partially obliterating his view in his outside mirror. The psychedelic truck was pulling up beside him before he saw it clearly. He sure hoped no one noticed who or what he was keeping company with! One look at Layla's rig and his cousins would tease him unmercifully, especially Travis and Peter. Of course, Fiona had seen them leave together so the whole town would be privy to that interesting information before long.

Grumbling under his breath, Michael eased out into traffic. A big gray dog rode beside Layla. That was not good. His German shepherd, King, was very territorial. It had taken him weeks to get King to accept Molly, the Australian shepherd he'd bought for herding.

He pondered his options. Since Layla was traveling with the dog he had a ready-made excuse to thank her politely for her time, pay her off as soon as the crisis was over and bid her a permanent goodbye.

Leading the way up Fourth Street, he noted the Colorado Springs Impressionist Museum on his right. How incongruous the minimalist structure looked in comparison to seasoned buildings like the Stagecoach Café.

As he passed, Michael saw Dahlia Sainsbury, the museum director, stepping from her silver BMW. That woman looked every bit as out of place as her museum did. It wasn't just her British accent or fancy designer clothes that put him off, either. There was something about her haughty attitude and her dark, incomprehensible gaze that gave him chills every time he encountered her.

He blinked, chanced another quick glance in his rearview mirror. A truck similar to his was pulling into the museum lot and coming to a stop beside Dahlia's car. The driver looked familiar. Was that where Hector had disappeared to?

Naw. Michael shook his head as he dismissed the silly notion. The last place he'd expect his new ranch foreman to visit was an art museum.

Sunlight reflecting off the thin layer of snow blanketing the countryside made Layla squint till her head started to ache. She reached over to pet the blue heeler. "Good boy, Smokey. We're almost there."

The mottled gray dog panted and licked her hand.

"I love you, too," Layla said. "We're going to like it out in the country. Lots of room for you to run and play." She smiled. "Me, too. I'm getting tired of being cooped up in this truck day after day. I could use a break."

Ahead of her, Michael slowed while passing the main ranch house. Two dogs, a giant German shepherd and a smaller Australian shepherd ran out to greet his truck. The brown-and-black shepherd loped alongside while the pretty little gray-and-white Aussie reverted to its inherent tendencies and tried to herd their two-vehicle convoy as if they were stray sheep.

Layla was relieved when they finally stopped in front of a large barn. She shut Smokey in her truck and called to Michael, "I like your welcoming committee."

"Thanks." He eyed her truck. "I'm glad you didn't let your dog out. King doesn't like strangers."

"Human or animal strangers?" she asked.

"Both." He grasped the shepherd's collar. "Come here and I'll introduce you."

"Let him go," Layla said. "He won't hurt me."

"You don't know that. He still hasn't taken to my new foreman and Hector's worked for me for months."

She was approaching calmly, confidently, and speaking in a quiet voice in spite of the dog's barking. "Hello, King. What a good boy you are."

King lunged against Michael's restraint. Layla paused. "Listen. Can't you hear the change in his bark? It was like a whiny yap when he started. Now it's deeper. Let him go before he gets any more defensive."

She held out her hand to the Aussie that was already sniffing her and wiggling at her feet like a happy puppy begging for affection. "And what's your name?"

"That's Molly," Michael said. "Okay. Look out. I'm turning King loose."

Layla braced herself and began to sing softly. The shepherd was on her in three bounds. She didn't flinch, even when shy Molly ducked behind her to escape King's wild rush. She was ready to raise her knee and knock him off balance if he decided to leap at her but that wasn't necessary. He slid to a stop, cocked his head to listen to her crooning, then sat at her feet as if he'd been trained to do so.

"Good boy." She let him sniff her fingers. In seconds, she was scratching behind his ears and he was leaning into her touch with his eyes half-closed.

Michael stared. "I don't believe it. If he was a cat he'd be purring."

"I told you I had a way with animals," Layla said. "Now, let's go see about that heifer, shall we?"

Following Michael into the barn she couldn't help admiring him. *For his caring heart,* she quickly told herself. Not that he was hard to look at. There was a rugged handsomeness about the rancher that appealed to her in a way that a lush spring meadow or a well-conditioned animal did. He moved like an athlete, graceful because he had control of his muscles, not because there was anything effete about him. On the contrary, he was masculine to the core. Yet he also radiated an unmistakable tenderness. Remembering his casual references to God and his apparent knowledge of Scripture, she assumed he was a fellow believer.

Layla smiled. The man's view of Christianity was probably far different than hers, even though they worshipped the same God. In her mind, she was more the earthy, sandals-wearing type, like Jesus had been when He was on earth. Michael Vance looked more like one of the stiff pew-warmers she'd encountered often in her travels. How sad for him.

Michael led Layla into the barn, the dogs at their heels. A thin ranch hand with a handlebar mustache and kind eyes stood waiting beside a stall.

"This is Norberto," Michael said. The astonished look on the older man's leathered face made Michael grin. "Norberto Cortez, meet our new vet, Layla Dixon."

"Ai-yi-yi." Norberto whistled between his teeth. "You surprise me, boss."

"I surprise myself," Michael admitted. "When I heard Doc Pritchard was out of town I figured we'd be on our own. Layla—Dr. Dixon—just happened to stop in at Fiona's while I was there. One thing led to another."

"So, I see."

His ranch hand looked far too pleased with himself to suit Michael. "She's here in an official capacity, to help the heifer." He glanced at the stall. "How's it going?"

Norberto shrugged. "I don't know. Not good, I think. She won't let me get close enough to look."

"Let me see what I can do," Layla said, stepping forward.

Michael was right beside her. "You're not going in there by yourself."

"Who says?"

"I do."

"Fine." She stood her ground, hands on her hips. "You go check on the calf and let me know if it's breech or not."

Making a face, Michael backed down. "Okay. You

can go in alone if you promise to be careful. We'll be right out here if you need us." Layla was already at the divided door of the stall, peering over the lower half that remained closed. He heard her speaking quietly. She paused for a few seconds, then eased the door open and stepped through.

Silence hung in the air like a cloud of winter fog. Michael crept closer. To his amazement, Layla already had one arm draped over the red-and-white heifer's neck and seemed to be mumbling something into its ear. Her lips were close enough that her breath was tickling the fine hairs inside the animal's ear and making it twitch.

He gestured to Norberto. "Look. You aren't going to believe this."

The older man nodded. "I have to believe it, boss. I see it."

Layla looked up. "You guys can come in now. Just take it easy. No fast moves." She placed the flat of her free hand on the cow's taut side below the deep concaves of the hide covering its hip bones. "She's in trouble, all right. The sooner we get her baby straightened out and pulled, the better her chances."

"I suppose she told you all that," Michael remarked, a little peeved that he and his best worker hadn't been able to calm the frightened animal the way this unusual woman had. "I heard you mumbling something to her but I never heard her say a thing to you."

"Mumbling, whispering, whatever. You didn't hear her because you weren't listening," Layla replied. Michael had shed his good leather coat and was rolling up his sleeves. His touch on the heifer's side made the animal flick its tail but it remained stationary. "That's right, girl," Layla said tenderly. "It's okay. We're here to help you. All of us. Even these ugly old cowboys."

Norberto chuckled under his breath as he bent down to inspect the business end of the cow, then sobered. "It's breech, boss. You want me to try for the legs or shall I let the doc do it?"

"Better leave our cow mumbler right where she is, at least till we get further along," Michael said. He looked to Layla. "That okay with you?"

Her grin was wide, her blue eyes sparkling. "Suits me. You two have probably pulled a lot more calves than I have. I defer to experience." She glanced down at her outfit. "Besides, I'm not dressed for barn duty —not that that would stop me if I was needed."

Already assisting Norberto, Michael barely glanced at her as he said, "I'm beginning to get the idea that nothing stops you once you make up your mind."

She laughed quietly. Michael was positive he heard her murmur, "Smart man."

The calf was soon born and wobbling around on gangly legs. To Layla's chagrin, its wild-eyed mama regarded it as an alien monster she wanted nothing to do with.

"That happens, especially with first-time mothers," Michael said. "She'll probably settle down and accept it soon. If not, we'll give it a bottle of colostrum. I keep some frozen for emergencies."

"I'll stay and work with her," Layla said. "I don't want her to get scared and step on her poor baby."

"She won't. We'll take it away and dry it so it doesn't get a chill, then bring it back and try again."

"Good idea." Layla shivered. "It is getting pretty cold. Must be almost dark."

"It's closer to eight," Michael said. "That's why I sent Norberto home. His wife, Imelda, has a sprained ankle and she needs him."

"Oh." Layla yawned. "No wonder I'm so tired. It's been a long day."

"Where are you staying?" Michael asked. "What motel?"

"I hadn't gotten around to renting a room when I stopped to eat." Truthfully, once she'd become involved with Michael Vance, little else had crossed her mind. "Don't worry. I can bed down out here with Winona."

"With who?" Michael's brow furrowed.

"Winona. Your cow. That's her name."

"The kid who raised her called her Cripple Creek Sunset Princess, or something like that. Where'd you get Winona?"

"She likes it best," Layla said, giggling at the flabbergasted look on his face. "You name your dogs. Why not the other animals?"

"I run between two hundred and two hundred-fifty head, depending on the season. Numbered ear tags are much more sensible."

"But not nearly as much fun," Layla countered.

"Ranching isn't a game. It's a business."

Michael threw a large bath towel over the calf and picked it up by closing his arms around it with all four of its long legs gathered together and hanging down.

Layla held the stall door open for him and followed him out, closing it behind her. "Where to, now?"

"Up to the house. It's warmer there. It's been six or seven hours since we ate and I'm starving. Can you cook?"

"Yes. Why?"

"Because I need a housekeeper worse than I need an on-site veterinarian. It wouldn't be a permanent job. Just till Imelda gets back on her feet. What do you say?"

"Well, I—"

"You could look after Winona, too. As long as you got meals on the table for me and a few of the hands and kept the place fairly clean, you could have all the rest of the time off to play with the livestock."

"I don't know. I don't think I'd like sleeping in the barn for very many nights. And I'm *not* the kind of girl who'd move in with you, no matter what my upbringing leads you to believe."

Michael's hands were full so he pointed with a nod of his head. "Grab my jacket, will you? We'll walk to the house."

"I said, I don't think it's right for us to sleep under the same roof."

"I heard you. I agree. I've got an empty cabin a little ways out. You can have that. It'll give you some privacy. You can even turn your dog loose out there as long as King doesn't get wind of him."

Layla gasped. "Oh, no! Poor Smokey. I forgot all about him." She peered into the dimness. "Where'd your dogs go?"

"I sent them home with Norberto," Michael said. "Let your dog out before he destroys your truck and come on. This soggy little guy is getting heavy."

She wanted to say, "You're a sweetheart," but thought better of it. Instead, she told him, "Okay. It's a deal. You've got yourself a temporary cook. Smokey and I will be honored to work on the Double V."

Chapter Three

Layla, Michael and the wobbly calf were together on the kitchen floor. Smokey lay under the table, snoring.

"I think his head and ears are dry enough," she said, cupping the calf's rust red and white face in her hands. "How are you coming with the rest of him?"

"Fine. I'm about ready to take him back to his mother and see how she's doing."

Layla got to her feet. "I'll go with you."

"I'd rather you stayed here and made us something to eat," Michael said.

"Okay, but..." A distant knocking drew her attention. "I think you have company."

"The timing could be better." He steadied the calf on the slippery floor. "Do you mind answering the door."

"Not at all. Take good care of Wilbur. I'll be right back." Whirling and starting for the front of the house, she giggled when she heard her new boss mutter, "Wilbur?"

The knocking persisted. A woman's voice called, "Michael? It's me."

Layla opened the door. On the porch stood a short, thin, graying woman holding a casserole dish. She reminded Layla of a grammar school teacher she'd once had.

"Hello," Layla said brightly. "Michael's busy in the kitchen." She swung the door wide. "Won't you come in?"

The other woman's brown eyes widened. She didn't move.

"Here, let me help you with that." Layla reached for the covered dish. "It must be heavy. Umm, it smells delicious. Italian?"

"Yes."

Recovering her composure the woman breezed past, leaving Layla to follow. She heard an exclamation seconds before she, too, reached the kitchen. It sounded like her new boss was getting scolded, big-time.

"Michael Vance," the woman shouted. "Look at this floor. I don't believe you did it again. What do you think barns are for? *That's* where you're supposed to keep your livestock, not in the house! Your grandfather must be turning over in his grave."

"I doubt it, Mom." He smiled sheepishly and gestured. "Layla Dixon, I'd like you to meet my mother, Marilyn. Mom works for the *Colorado Springs Sentinel.*"

"Pleased to meet you, Mrs. Vance." Carefully placing the casserole on the table she held out her hand.

Marilyn shook it briefly, then glared at her son once more. "I guess I was misinformed. I heard you were all alone out here and needed a decent meal so I brought you some of your aunt Lidia's lasagna. Guess you won't be needing it after all." One thin eyebrow arched.

"We'd love to have it, wouldn't we, *Doctor?*"

This situation was getting funnier and funnier. Marilyn was letting her son know in no uncertain terms that she didn't approve of his housekeeping or his guest, and Michael was doing his best to explain without actually copping a plea the way he would have as a boy. It was all Layla could do to keep from giggling.

Marilyn stared, first at Michael, then at Layla, plainly giving her the once over before she asked, "Doctor? Is somebody sick?"

"Dr. Dixon is a vet," Michael explained. "She came to help with a difficult calving."

"That's right," Layla added with her sweetest smile. "The cow delivered and I'm happy to report Wilbur is doing just fine, too."

"Who's Wilbur?" Marilyn scowled at her son. "I thought your new foreman was named Hector."

Cheeks reddening, lips pressed together, Michael looked as if he was trying not to laugh. His struggles were so comical Layla made a muted, chortling noise, which led Michael to sound like he was strangling as he choked back a snort. Their gazes met. Mischief twinkled in their eyes. Together, they erupted into riotous laughter that brought Smokey out of his hidey-hole and into the fray.

"Will somebody please tell me what's so funny?" Marilyn insisted. "And when did you get another dog?"

Michael was the first to regain his self-control. "Wilbur's this calf, not my foreman," he said. "The doc here likes to name all the critters she treats. Smokey's her dog."

"Oh." Marilyn's tone became conciliatory. "How nice. I hope you like lasagna, my dear. Michael's aunt Lidia is famous for her authentic Italian cooking."

"I'm sure it will be wonderful," Layla said, hoping against hope that it was a vegetarian dish and doubting it very much. "Before we eat, I think we should take Wilbur back to his mama and see if we can get him to nurse, don't you, Mr. Vance?"

"Actually, I was about to suggest that," Michael said. "After we put him in the barn, I think Dr. Dixon and I should take turns eating so one of us can stay with the pair and get them used to each other." He shot a quick glance at the casserole, then winked at Layla.

She understood immediately. "Right. I'll take the first shift so you can visit with your mother. Let's go, Smokey."

Michael hoisted the calf and followed, still chuckling quietly.

* * *

"I mopped the floor while you were gone," Marilyn told him when he returned.

"You didn't need to do that, Mom."

"I know. I'm glad your veterinarian decided to give us this chance to talk," she said, dishing up a plate of lasagna for her son. "I wanted to tell you what I heard about Fiona's boy."

"Which one? Brendan or Quinn?"

She put the plate on the table. "Brendan."

Marilyn had lowered her voice even though they were alone, leading Michael to suspect she was about to tell him something she shouldn't know in the first place.

"Fiona says the FBI is investigating the attempt on Uncle Max's life. And guess who they've been watching?"

"I don't have a clue. Aren't you going to eat with me?"

"You go ahead. I had supper hours ago." She took a chair next to Michael and leaned closer. "Owen Frost!"

"The deputy mayor? No way!"

"Yes. Before Max was shot, he'd mentioned to Lidia that he thought Owen was acting funny. Lidia told Brendan and he passed the word to his superiors."

"That doesn't make the man guilty. Owen's had a rough personal life. Maybe he's having trouble dealing with it."

"Ha! No wonder. Even his own daughter won't

have anything to do with him. Why do you think Jenna left town?"

"Are you sure you have your facts straight, Mom? Brendan's a great kidder."

"I don't think he'd joke about something this serious, especially not to his own mother." Marilyn's forehead knit. "I'll have to ask Fiona for more details."

"You've been hanging around that newspaper office too long," Michael said. "You're beginning to snoop like Colleen Montgomery."

"Nonsense. There's not a reporter's bone in my body." Marilyn rose. "Have you had your fill? Shall I dish up some for the doctor? I could take it to her." She paused, smiled. "Or *you* could."

"Later." Michael was stalling. No sense hurting his mother's feelings by revealing that the beef-filled lasagna was not something Layla would knowingly eat. "Right now, I'd better go check the cabin, make sure it's livable and light the fireplace to warm it up faster."

"The cabin? Why?"

"I've offered it to Dr. Dixon while she's working here." He gave his mother a lopsided smile. "You didn't think I was going to let her move in here with me, did you?"

"Perish the thought."

"Exactly. Pastor Gabriel would be knocking on my door, Bible in hand, in a heartbeat if I pulled a stunt like that." His grin widened. "So would you."

"Your father would be proud of the man you've become," Marilyn said quietly. "I know I am."

"Except for the calf in the kitchen?"

She laughed. "Nobody's perfect."

Even though Layla had snacked on granola for energy, she was so weary by the time they finished in the barn and Michael showed her to her cabin, she barely noticed how cozy the compact dwelling was. She paused on a rag rug just inside the door to remove her boots while her blue heeler sniffed his way across the room.

"The bedroom is up there. In the loft." He pointed.

Layla's eyes widened. "Whoa! I have to climb a ladder?"

"I like to think of it as a very steep stairway," he said. "If you get up at night, you'd be wise to turn on a light. Even though there's a railing, I'd hate to see you make a misstep and fall off the edge."

"Yeah, so would I," Layla said cynically. "Any reason why I couldn't just sleep down here on the couch?"

"None that I can think of, as long as you're comfortable. I imagine Smokey would prefer to stay off ladders, too."

"Probably so." She sighed and plopped onto the sofa. "Mind if I put my feet up on the coffee table?"

"Make yourself at home."

"Thanks. I'm not used to wearing those boots. I'm more a moccasin kind of person."

"I thought you were going to say you preferred going barefoot."

"Not in the winter. I may be free-spirited but I'm

not crazy." She glanced past him at the ladder leading to the loft. Crazy would be to climb that thing when she felt queasy just thinking of it. Getting up on a chair was about as high as she could stand without succumbing to dizziness. That weakness, however, was not one she felt the need to reveal to her host.

Michael put down her suitcase and backed toward the door. "Well, then, I'll say good night. Get some shut-eye. The hands and I usually eat about seven, after morning chores. Dorothy used to start baking before dawn but Imelda never got going that early."

"Refresh my memory. Who's Dorothy?"

"Dorothy kept house and cooked for the Double V for years. She retired last year. I hired Imelda to take her place because her husband, Norberto, already worked for me. I thought it would be good for them both." Michael grimaced. "I just hadn't counted on her getting hurt and distracting him from his regular chores."

Layla was nodding. "Okay. Got it. Breakfast at seven." She yawned and covered her mouth. "I usually have a handful of granola and some yogurt. I don't suppose that's the kind of breakfast you have in mind."

"Not hardly. You can look over the grocery supplies and make out an order list tomorrow. In the meantime, I know there are plenty of fresh eggs in the refrigerator. You do eat those, don't you?"

Layla nodded and yawned again. "I'm what they call an ovo-lacto vegetarian. I eat eggs and dairy products."

"That's comforting. Would it kill you to fry a little ham to go with the eggs?"

"It wouldn't hurt me nearly as much as it did the pig," Layla quipped. "How about an omelet?"

"Okay. Whatever. Just hot food and plenty of it. Plan on a maximum of six. Some of the men have been fending for themselves and doing their own cooking since Imelda got hurt, so I'm not sure how many will show up. We can discuss the week's menus in the morning, after you've had a chance to look over the pantry."

"Um-hum." Layla bit back the urge to quit the job then and there. When the rancher had asked her if she could cook, she hadn't thought it would be for a horde of hungry men. Most of her meals were eaten raw. How in the world was she going to please a bunch of guys whose idea of a good cook was anyone who could char a hunk of some poor defenseless animal to their taste?

She opened her mouth to ask Michael if he had any tofu in his refrigerator, then decided against it, said, "Good night," and watched him depart.

Smokey came up and laid his head on her lap as soon as they were alone. She scratched behind his pendulous ears. "I've fallen in with a bunch of carnivores," she told the dog. "Your kind of people. The table scraps around here should please you more than mine do. Ugh."

He thumped his tail against the couch as if he understood and sympathized.

Layla smiled. "It's okay, baby. I can stand almost anything for a little while. We won't be here for long."

When Michael entered the ranch house kitchen the following morning he was greeted by a scene that nearly made him burst out laughing.

Layla had tied her hair back with a ribbon, which was just as well, since she had flour from her fingertips to her elbows, dusted on her cheeks, and spotting her makeshift apron. The dining table wasn't set because she'd apparently rolled out her biscuit dough there and had yet to clean up the residue.

"Something smells great," Michael said.

Layla whirled. "Oh, no! Is it seven already?"

He checked his watch. "Actually, it's ten after. Don't worry. Norberto's gone to fix Imelda breakfast and the other men have already eaten. It's just you and me. And maybe my foreman, Hector Delgato. I haven't talked to him this morning so I'm not sure."

"Whew!" Layla drew the back of her hand across her forehead, leaving more white streaks behind. "That's a relief. I was afraid I was going to have to start frying eggs before I got this mess cleaned up."

One of Michael's eyebrows arched. "You do get into your work, don't you?"

That brought a grin. "If something is worth doing, it's worth doing all-out."

"So, I see." His glance briefly rested on the remains of her biscuit-making project, then traveled back to her. "Looks like you got dough on your necklace."

"I know. I took my bracelets off before I started. I guess I'm going to have to leave my other jewelry for later next time, too." Blue eyes twinkling, she looked into his darker gaze. "I hate that. I don't feel normal without it."

"I like it, too."

"My jewelry? You do?"

"Sure. You jingle. I can always hear you coming."

"Kind of like belling a cat, you mean?" Layla was wiping down the table, trying to gather the loose flour and little globs of dough as she talked.

"You could put it that way." Michael paused as they were joined by a third party. "Hector. I wondered if you'd make it back for breakfast. Norberto said you were checking the south fence."

"I was," the other man said. Though he answered Michael, his attention was on Layla. Michael didn't like the way he was obviously sizing her up.

"Dr. Dixon, this is Hector Delgato, my foreman," Michael said.

"Pleased to meet you." Layla smiled amiably and held up her floury fingers. "I'd shake hands, but…"

"Doctor? Of what, biscuits?" Hector said with a smirk.

"This morning, I am," she replied. "When I'm not up to my elbows in food, I'm a veterinarian."

"I see."

Michael watched, curious, as his foreman's expression became unreadable. Where before he'd seemed lecherous and snide, he now appeared put off. Perhaps he was one of those egotistical men who didn't approve of educated women. It was entirely possible. Michael knew too little about him personally to judge.

"I just stopped in to tell you I fixed the fence," Hector told him, pointedly ignoring Layla. "I need to run into town. We're out of calf supplement."

"You're not staying to eat?" Michael asked.

"No. Not interested. Too much to do."

"Okay. See you later."

Michael watched Hector leave, then turned to Layla. "I'm sorry he was so abrupt. I don't know what got into him. Guess you scared him."

"Me? How?"

"By being a college grad and a vet to boot, I suppose. Hector came with good references but he doesn't have a fancy degree to prove how smart he is."

"It's not just that," she said thoughtfully. "There was something else that bothered me."

"Like what? His voice is always kind of raspy."

"I don't think it was that." She carried her washrag to the sink and rinsed it out before returning to the table. "His eyes, maybe? I really can't say. I'll tell you one thing, though. If he was a dog, I'd think twice before I'd turn my back on him. He's—"

She hesitated. Sniffed. Straightened. "Do you smell smoke? Oh, no! My biscuits!"

Michael got to the oven first and yanked open the door. The room immediately filled with so much smoke the alarm on the ceiling in the hall began to wail.

He grabbed a couple of pot holders and lifted the pan filled with the charred remains.

"Are they edible?" she shouted over the pulsing squeal of the ongoing alarm.

"Not in my book. Open the back door, will you? I'll take them outside so they stop making that stupid alarm go crazy."

As he passed, she sheepishly asked, "How do you like your eggs?"

Michael was coughing and laughing too hard to answer.

The private line rang in the office. The voice was familiar. And expected. "Good morning, Chief."

"Don't call me Chief," *El Jefe* growled into the phone.

"What should I call you, then? Escalante?"

"No. I told you to never use that name again."

"Sorry. What's wrong? Is there a problem with the shipment?"

"I hope not. It should arrive in the States tomorrow. Once it's in the tunnels and our men have cut it for the street, I'll feel better."

"Just keep telling yourself how filthy rich you and I are going to be."

"Among other things." He cleared his throat. "I have some unexpected details to see to today. Don't look for me until after the shipment arrives."

"What's so important that you'd stay away when such a big deal is going down? The others in the cartel won't like that."

"It can't be helped. I heard Vance found himself a new veterinarian."

"So?"

"So, I intend to look up her background and see where she went to school, where she's worked. I don't want anybody to figure out what's going on with his cattle before I'm ready."

"You going to lay off for a while?"

El Jefe cursed. "I wish I could. I poisoned another batch yesterday. They haven't died yet but they will."

"And then?"

"Then, we'll find out how good at her job the pretty doctor is. If it looks like she's on to me, she'll have to have an accident."

"Fatal?"

Laughing, *El Jefe* said, "I certainly hope so."

Chapter Four

Layla was cleaning up after breakfast when Marilyn showed up again, this time at the back door.

"Morning," Layla called out. "I think Michael's gone to the barn with Norberto."

"Good morning, yourself. Actually, I wasn't looking for Michael." She stepped aside and gestured proudly. "I brought someone to meet you. This is my daughter, Holly."

Layla smiled. Mama had brought reinforcements this time. How funny! She dried her hands and held one out to the willowy brunette. "Pleased to meet you. I'm Layla Dixon."

Returning her smile, Holly asked, "DVM?"

"That's what my diploma says. I still can't get used to being called Dr. Dixon, though. Just call me Layla."

"I'm Holly Montgomery. Mom keeps forgetting I'm not a Vance anymore. Jake and I were married the same time Peter and Emily were."

"I'm afraid you've lost me there," Layla said. "I haven't lived around here for years. I'm not up on the latest gossip."

"Just as well," Holly said, laughing lightly. "There are way too many Vances and Montgomerys anyway. If I hadn't been raised in Colorado Springs I'd get the relationships confused, too."

Marilyn had remained near the door. "We just stopped by to pick up Lidia's casserole dish. While you two girls get acquainted, I think I'll run out and say hello to Michael."

Giggling, Holly shook her head as her mother beat a hasty retreat. "Subtle, isn't she?"

"Not really. Did I scare her that much last night?"

"You floored her," Holly admitted. "My brother hasn't had a girlfriend since Tammy broke his heart and headed for California to be a movie star."

"Takes all kinds," Layla said. "But I'm not anybody's girlfriend. I really was hired to fill in for Imelda and help with the livestock."

"I believe you. Mom, however, has already started imagining you and my big brother as a couple."

Thoughtful and sympathetic, Layla took the opportunity to ask more about her boss's past. "I can't imagine anyone choosing Hollywood over the peacefulness and beauty of this country." *Let alone jilting Michael Vance.* "Maybe Tammy will change her mind and come back."

"Not likely. She actually landed a part on a soap opera, in spite of having virtually no acting experience except for a few school plays."

"That's amazing. I thought it was supposed to be next to impossible to break into show business."

"It is. Tammy knew what she wanted and went after it. That's more than I can say for Mike."

Layla shook her head. "You're wrong there. Michael—I mean Mr. Vance—knows exactly what he wants and puts his whole heart into it."

"This ranch, you mean?"

"Yes. How long has he owned it?"

"It's been in our family since Grandpa Bennett bought it from Frank Montgomery Sr. to bail him out of debt. That was back in the forties. Bennett's the one responsible for building Vance Memorial Hospital."

"Now I know why that name sounded familiar. The hospital was already in operation when I was a kid."

"Right. If the Montgomerys hadn't sold this ranch and moved to Colorado Springs to start over, my Jake's folks might never have met. It's actually pretty incredible when you think about it." She grinned. "So is your showing up at Fiona's just when my brother needed a vet."

"He'd have found someone else if I hadn't been there. The phone book is full of veterinary practices."

"True. And I'm sure they're fine doctors. But he didn't know any of them well enough to feel comfortable confiding his deep dark secrets."

Layla's forehead knit. "What deep dark secrets?"

"Uh-oh. I'm in trouble now." Holly groaned. "Mike's going to kill me." She backed toward the door, groping for the handle. "Well, gotta go. See you later."

"Holly, what—"

Protesting was useless. The younger woman was already outside and hurrying toward the barn. What could she have meant? Layla wondered. What kind of terrible secrets could Michael Vance have that he needed to hide from local veterinarians?

Layla shivered. Several possibilities came to mind, none of them minor. What had she gotten herself into?

Waiting until Marilyn and Holly drove away, Layla made a beeline for the main barn. The sooner she had it out with Michael, the better. If, as she suspected, he was trying to hide a communicable bovine disease, she was going straight to the authorities.

She found him talking to Hector, so she stood back till the men were through and the foreman had left.

Michael smiled. "Hi, Doc. I hear you met my baby sister."

"Yes." Though Layla tried to hide her displeasure, she could tell from Michael's changing expression that he was sensing something amiss.

He sobered. "What's wrong? My mother didn't insult you, did she?"

"No. She was very pleasant."

"I know Holly wouldn't get out of line. She's the sweetest one of the bunch."

"She did mention something that has me worried.

How long were you going to wait before you told me your cattle are sick?"

"They're not." Michael's jaw muscles knotted, his hands curling into fists. "At least I don't think so."

"Then what did your sister mean about you having a deep, dark secret that involved needing the services of a veterinarian?"

Stepping closer to her, he gestured toward a stack of hay bales. "Have a seat. It's a long story."

Layla perched on the farthest edge of the bottom row of bales, hoping he wouldn't crowd her. She'd been trembling ever since Holly's slip of the tongue and didn't want Michael's nearness to make her nervousness worse. It was one thing to admire his rugged good looks from a distance and quite another to let him get too close for comfort. No matter what his mother thought, she was not about to take her attraction to the rancher seriously. They were as unsuited to each other as any couple she'd ever met.

Layla's active imagination compared them to Beauty and the Beast, with a slight modification. They were more an Appreciator of Beauty and a Consumer of Beasts. Totally mismatched. To her relief, Michael sat down two bales away.

He sighed. "It all started about three months ago."

"Three months! And you're just getting around to looking into it? I don't believe this."

"Hear me out before you jump to conclusions. Why do you think I didn't want word to get out? That's exactly the kind of reaction I'd expected from the public. You're a professional. You should want to know all the facts before you panic."

"I'm not panicking," Layla argued. "Okay. I'm listening. Talk. And it had better be good."

"There was, and is, no sign of disease. None. The affected animals were born and raised right here so I know I haven't imported anything infectious. They looked fine one day and were dying the next."

"How many?"

"Five, to start with. They were healthy cows that had missed their last breeding. We'd brought them up to the squeeze chutes to check them and change their ear tags before we sent them to the sale barn." He made a face. "Sorry. I know you don't approve but that's how it was."

"My lifestyle is my choice," Layla said. "I don't insist everybody stop eating meat just because I prefer not to. Go on. What happened then?"

"We gave them a ration of hay and a little grain and left them penned up for the night. Norberto checked on them after supper and noticed a few of them down but he didn't think anything of it. It's not unusual for the herd to bed down to chew their cud." He grimaced. "I suppose you know that. I'm not being condescending. I just don't want to leave out any details."

"You're doing fine." Layla propped one foot on the hay and laced her fingers together around that knee while she concentrated.

"In the morning, two of the cows were already dead and the others were failing. Yet there wasn't a mark on them. Nothing."

"Scours? Dehydration?"

"They were real thirsty, those that could stand long enough to drink. They didn't last long."

"What did you do then?"

"Called Doc Pritchard. He came out and took tissue samples before we bulldozed a big hole and buried everything. The lab results came back negative."

"You sterilized the pen, the fences?"

Michael nodded. "Yes. Even disposed of the top layers of dirt."

"Has the problem recurred?"

"Yes." Michael got to his feet and began to pace in front of her. "That was what brought me into town the other day. I was looking for Pritchard. He's apparently on an extended leave of absence."

"So," Layla said thoughtfully, "that's what Holly meant. You're not hiding the losses. Your regular vet *does* know but he's currently unavailable."

"Exactly. What I don't want to do is start a big panic over this. I've kept my cattle isolated since the first deaths so I know they haven't spread anything, but there's no way I can prove it. The last time U.S. beef was suspected of being tainted, over thirty countries closed their borders to our meat exports."

"I know." Layla, too, stood and began to walk back and forth. "Okay. Here's what we'll do. I'll go over the results of the lab tests on the first batch you lost." She paused. "I take it you've already buried the latest casualties."

"No. The ground was frozen too hard. I had

Hector push the remains into a pile and burn them. It was all I could do, under the circumstances."

"So we won't be getting samples there," Layla said. "Are any other animals showing signs of illness?"

"Not yet." He removed his hat and raked his fingers through his hair. "I'm at the end of my rope, Doc. I could lose everything and never know what hit me."

"That's not an option," Layla said firmly. "We'll find an answer." Forgetting herself, she hesitated by his side and laid her hand gently on his forearm. "I promise."

Not until Michael's gaze met hers did she realize how poignant, how personal, the moment had become.

Quickly pulling away, Layla stepped back and busied herself by brushing bits of straw off her long skirt. She could still feel a tingle on her fingertips where she'd touched him, even though he was wearing a jacket. Her cheeks warmed. She averted her face to hide the telling reaction.

"You're not going to the authorities?" he asked.

Surprised, Layla looked up at him. "I'd report this in a minute if I thought there was a danger to other ranches. Right off, I can't think of a single germ that would cause the symptoms you've described. I hate to say this, Mr. Vance, but I suspect your stock may have been poisoned."

"That's impossible!"

"Have you got a better idea?"

He shook his head. "No. Tell me what to do next and I'll do it."

"I'll want to take clean samples of all the feed and hay." Glancing at the stall where Winona was starting to settle down with her calf, Layla felt her heart speed. "And don't add anything new to any pens till we've had it checked. Your stock is better off hungry than dead."

"My men are scrupulously careful. We use very little pesticide. And when we do, we make sure no livestock is in the vicinity."

"What if this was done on purpose? Is that possible?"

Michael nodded soberly. "Unfortunately, yes. My old foreman disappeared about the time my losses began. At first, I thought maybe Ben had fallen off the wagon and was on a drinking binge or doing drugs again. When he didn't come back, I started to wonder if he'd been responsible for the deaths. The only problem is, he didn't have a motive."

"He wasn't upset with you?"

"He sure shouldn't have been. I gave him a chance when a lot of ranchers wouldn't even talk to him. He was a good worker. I was positive he was going to stay clean and sober this time."

Pensive, Layla fiddled with one of her many earrings. She always thought more clearly when she was fingering her jewelry. Her mother had often joked that she'd be mute if she didn't wear all that silver to spur her ideas.

"Could he sneak back onto the Double V without someone spotting him?"

"I suppose so. It's a big place." Michael scowled. "Do you really think that's what's wrong?"

"I don't know yet," Layla answered. "Show me the place where the last cattle died. I want to see it for myself."

The empty cattle pen was as barren and bleak as the winter hills. A dusting of snow covered the ground. Layla opened the gate and walked in, her feet crunching through the thin crust of ice that had formed from partially melted snow when the temperature had dropped.

"They were all right here?" she asked Michael.

"Yes. Both times we'd brought in a small group. When Norberto checked the following morning, they were already acting sick."

"Only them? None of the others they had been with before you cut them out?"

"Not that I've seen. My herd is pretty big. We drive them down to this lower elevation in the winter and keep them in pastures so we can supplement their feed. The weather is too harsh on the open range."

"I'll want to check every animal on the ranch, including the horses. If you have any more range cattle penned up I'll start with them."

"Norberto put a few head over by his place so he could keep a better eye on them, maybe catch on to what was wrong."

"Then that's where I want to start," Layla said.

"The Cortez family has their own place on Double V land. It's not far. I'll drive you."

"Okay. Shut the dogs in the barn with Winona and Wilbur to keep them from following and let's go."

A truly pitiful sight greeted Layla and Michael when they pulled up next to the portable rail enclosure behind Norberto's modest home. Three steers were standing, heads down, sides heaving. A fourth lay crumpled in the snow, barely breathing.

Layla wasn't surprised to hear Michael curse under his breath. Death was clearly stalking these poor animals, too.

She climbed down from the truck and walked to the railing. When Michael joined her she said, "I'll get my medical bag. I'm afraid I can't offer much hope, though. Looks like the best we can do is make them a little more comfortable."

Layla eased the gate open and approached the suffering steers while speaking softly. "I'm so sorry, boys. I wish you could tell me what's wrong so I could help you."

She circled the bunched animals, assessing their condition before proceeding. They were dehydrated, yet from the looks of the pen, none of them had relieved themselves since the snowfall.

Hay lay in a jumbled, trampled pile at one end of the pen. Beside the water trough was a smaller, round pan that looked as if it had recently contained grain.

In their distress, the steers had apparently knocked the defroster out of their water and the trough had iced over. Layla punched through the thin layer in the hopes they might drink if they had the opportunity. None of them moved.

Cold puckered her wet fingers and made her wish she'd used a tool to break the ice instead of her fist. She stared at her patients. "What is it, Lord?" she prayed softly. "What's wrong? Help me see? Please?"

No voice of wisdom boomed from Heaven. Layla sighed. She'd prayed for animals and doctored them ever since she was a child. This time, however, she was totally stumped.

Chilled to the bone, she tucked her hands into the pockets of her down-filled vest and shivered. Everything was frozen. Icicles hung from the fence rails. The backs of the steers had collected snow, melted it with body heat and formed their own private icy torture. Even if she and Michael could coax them to walk to the barn, which she doubted in view of their present weakened condition, it wouldn't be a good idea. Winona and Wilbur were still healthy and happy. She couldn't take a chance of spreading possible contamination. Neither could Michael.

He broke into her thoughts to ask, "Shall we put them down? I hate to see them suffer."

Layla looked away, unwilling to admit defeat. There must be something. Some clue. Some… Her brow furrowed. The empty feed pan looked as if it had liquid in the bottom. Given the air temperature, that was impossible. Her glance darted from the pan to Michael Vance, then back to the pan.

"Where do you get these?" she asked, pointing.

"The feed tubs? They're not new, if that's what you mean."

Layla was bending over and feeling the bottom of the six-inch-deep pan. The wet substance was definitely not water. It was slippery, almost slimy. She held up her fingers and noted a greenish tinge.

"Do your men ever use them for anything else?"

"Like what?" Michael joined her.

"Like changing the antifreeze in your machinery." She showed him her fingers. "That's sure what this stuff looks like. And it would explain a lot. Ethylene glycol can be deadly. Dogs are usually the ones who are accidentally poisoned."

"You think that's what's wrong with my cattle?"

"There's a real good chance. I'll have to have this stuff tested but I think we have our poison. What we don't have is the answer to how it got here. Could your missing foreman have been careless enough to use these tubs to drain radiators into?"

Michael was shaking his head. "I don't know. If he did, why didn't Doc Pritchard notice?"

"Maybe because it wasn't this cold then. I only saw it because it wasn't frozen solid like everything else." She looked with pity on the suffering cattle. "There is no antidote at this stage. Once they begin to metabolize the toxins in their liver, their kidneys fail. It's always fatal. That's why people who care about the environment are trying to get manufacturers to change over to propylene glycol. It's a lot less lethal."

Chagrined, Michael nodded. "Okay. Go on back to the barn. I'll take care of things here."

Once again moved by his kindheartedness, she gently touched his shoulder with her clean hand. "I'm so sorry."

"At least we have some idea what's been happening and we can put a stop to it," he said. "Don't be sorry for that. I owe you plenty."

Layla reached for the empty feed pan and lifted it by its rolled rim. "I'll take this with me so nothing else gets into it. The stuff is sweet to the taste. That's why dogs lick it up if it's spilled on the ground."

"I know." Michael sighed. "I'd just never dreamed it would show up in my feed. How much does it take to kill an animal?"

"I don't know about cattle," she answered. "Three to four tablespoons of it will kill a big dog."

"How about diluted? It must have been thinned if Ben used some of these pans to drain out the old antifreeze and put in new for winter."

"Maybe the water evaporated," Layla said. "I'd have to do a little research to tell for sure." She paused by the side of his truck. "You sure you're going to be okay? I can stay and help if you want?"

"No. Go on. Take the truck. Norberto keeps a rifle in his barn. I'll walk home when I'm done."

Though she saw unshed tears glistening in his eyes, she respected his courage, got behind the wheel of his black truck and drove slowly away.

Half an hour later, Layla had scraped samples of the greenish residue into specimen bottles and labeled them. Stepping out onto the back porch to see if Michael had returned, she noticed a cloud of black smoke rising from the direction of the latest catastrophe. Michael was sterilizing the pen. Her heart went out to him. Ranching was hard on a person who cared about livestock the way he obviously did.

She sighed. The contaminated feed pan would have to be stored someplace where it wouldn't be accidentally put back into service and could be preserved as evidence in case a crime had actually been committed. Right now, it was relatively safe lying in the bed of his truck but she'd feel much better once it was totally secured.

Pensive and sad, Layla approached the ranch truck. She blinked. Gaped. *Wait a minute!* She'd left that tub right there. She knew she had. To do otherwise would have been unforgivably careless.

She stuck her hand into the truck's bed and felt around just to be sure she wasn't overlooking the round, shallow tub because it was also black. There was nothing there. Not even a hint that the contaminated feeder had ever existed.

Eyes wide, she scanned the empty yard. Her breath caught. Surely Michael's dogs hadn't carried it off!

Air whistled out of her lungs in relief moments later. The barn was still closed with King and Molly inside, and Smokey was snoozing in her cabin. Whatever had happened to the pan, it wasn't hurting the dogs. Not yet. But it was crucial to their future safety that she locate it.

An acrid odor drifted to her. Layla wrinkled her

nose, shaded her eyes and studied the distant fire. Her initial assumption was that the odor was coming from Michael's cleanup work. Now, she questioned that conclusion. Smoke from the Cortez place was drifting slowly to the west, while the main ranch house and barn sat almost due east. So what smelled so bad?

A faint wisp of smoke rose from the far side of the barn. Layla blinked. She would have missed noticing it if she hadn't been peering at everything so intently.

Without thinking, she started to run, screeching, "Norberto! Hector! Somebody, help! The barn's on fire!"

She rounded the corner and slid to a stop, gasping a heartfelt, "Thank You, God!" when she realized there was no immediate danger to animals or buildings.

A pile of soiled hay was doing its best to burn in spite of the frigid temperatures. Her first thought was spontaneous combustion. That wasn't a rare phenomenon in the heat of summer but it didn't fit this situation. A carelessly discarded cigarette was a far more probable source of ignition, especially this time of year.

She didn't like leaving the pile smoldering that close to a vulnerable building so she grabbed a pitchfork and proceeded to scatter the old hay to cool it.

The tines of the pitchfork hit something hard. Puzzled, Layla scraped away the glowing embers to reveal what had been buried in the fire. It was a black feed pan. She didn't have to look closely to see the scrape marks she'd left on it when she'd taken her lab samples.

One mystery was resolved. When someone had tried to destroy the evidence, they'd admitted to purposely poisoning Michael Vance's innocent cattle. What kind of monster would do a thing like that?

Chapter Five

Trembling, Layla quickly spun around, praying no one was lurking close by, ready to pounce on her. All she could think about was alerting Michael as soon as possible.

She pushed the pan around in the slushy snow to make sure it was cool enough to handle, then grabbed it by the rim and dashed for his truck.

The pitchfork stayed in her hand, just in case. It wasn't much of a defense weapon but it was better than nothing. Until she and Michael figured out what was going on, she intended to be prepared.

Tossing the pan and pitchfork into the back of the truck, she slid into the driver's seat, gunned the engine and whipped the wheel around till she was headed in the right direction. The rear wheels slipped then caught, spraying a rooster tail of mud and melted snow. Layla didn't care. She had to get to Michael, to warn him what they were up against.

Approaching the Cortez home, she saw Michael standing next to the fence with Norberto. They both looked startled when she barreled up to them and skidded to a stop.

Michael handed his shovel to Norberto and stomped over to Layla as she got out of the truck. "What do you think this is, the Indianapolis Speedway?"

She waved her hands in front of her like windshield wipers set on the fastest speed. "Never mind that. Listen. I know what's been happening."

"So do I," Michael retorted. "You've been driving like a maniac." He held out his hand. "Give me the keys."

"They're in the truck." Layla ignored his ire. "I was on the back porch and I saw a fire."

Michael rolled his eyes and glanced past Norberto at the smoldering pyre he'd lit to sterilize the area. "No kidding. Imagine that."

"Not *there*," Layla insisted. "Up by the barn."

That was all it took to set Michael in motion. He shoved her out of his way so he'd have access to the truck and started to get in.

Layla grabbed his arm in passing and hung on, forcing him to stop and listen. "It's okay. I put it out."

Although his posture relaxed a bit she could still feel tensed muscle beneath her grasp. "Calm down," she said. "It was just a little hay pile, back where we put the stuff that's cleaned out of the stalls."

"What happened?"

"Thankfully, I'd gone outside or we'd never know."

"I still don't," Michael barked. He motioned to Norberto. "Go see to it."

Layla held up both hands and shouted, "No! Nobody should go up there. There might be clues. The more we walk around the barn, the less there'll be for the police to find when they get here."

"You called the police?"

"Well, no, not yet. But when you see for yourself you'll probably want to. There was no way it could have been an accidental fire."

Michael was shaking his head and staring at her as if she were the dumbest city slicker he'd ever met. "Refuse like that naturally combusts all the time, Layla. The pile heats up by itself and if conditions are right, it starts to smolder."

"In the middle of winter?"

He arched an eyebrow. "You're right. But what makes you so sure it was arson?"

She released his arm slowly in case he decided to bolt. When he merely stood there, giving her his trademark cynical look, she stepped to the rear of the truck and retrieved the scorched black pan.

Displaying it, she said, "This does. After I took my samples into the house, I went back to get the pan out of the truck. I wanted to put it somewhere the dogs wouldn't bother it. It was gone."

She paused, waiting for the truth to sink into Michael Vance's thick skull. As his eyes widened, she added. "That's right. I found it buried in the middle of the burning pile. A few more minutes and there wouldn't have been any proof of how your cattle were poisoned. None."

"You're sure?"

She sighed. "Unfortunately, yes. I know I left the pan in the bed of this truck when I went into the house. Your dogs are still shut in the barn and mine is in my cabin. There's no way any of them took this away and buried it."

"Coyotes?" Norberto suggested.

Michael contradicted him. "Not this winter. Mice and rabbits are thick in the wild. Coyotes aren't starving like some years. There's nothing to lure them that close to the house." He began to scowl. "Besides, coyotes don't carry matches. It looks like we're dealing with another kind of predator. The two-legged kind."

He took the damaged feed pan from Layla and studied it. "You're sure this is the same one?"

"Positive." She pointed. "See? Those are the marks I made when I took the samples."

"And you left it in the truck?"

"Yes. I didn't want to take it into the house because it was so filthy."

"Where are the samples, now?"

"In your kitchen," she said, staring into the distance toward the main house. Her eyes widened. "Uh-oh. Are you thinking what I'm thinking?"

"Probably." Michael slid into the driver's seat while Layla ran to the passenger door. He shouted at Norberto. "Stay with this fire till you're sure your house is safe. We'll take care of the other one."

Layla jumped in, slammed the door and braced herself with one hand against the dashboard. "The samples are still there. They have to be."

"For all our sakes, I hope so," Michael said.

She agreed. If they lost her initial samples it would slow their investigation, maybe even end it. Whatever residue might be left in the pan after being burned was seriously contaminated, if not totally destroyed.

"I should have brought them with me," Layla said. "I'm so sorry. I didn't think."

"You put out the fire and saved the barn," Michael reasoned. "That's a point in your favor. Don't borrow trouble before we see for ourselves, okay?"

"Okay."

She knew she should heed his advice but her body refused to listen. Her heart was hammering so hard she was sure it would burst and she couldn't seem to catch her breath.

"Please, God," she whispered. "Please protect the evidence."

Please, please, please, echoed in her pounding head like a familiar tune that refuses to go away no matter how hard a person tries to silence it.

Layla quit struggling and let the simplistic prayer flow as it would. She was beyond reasonable thought. Beyond logic. All that mattered at that moment was getting her hands on those samples and making sure they were safe.

She was out of the truck and running before Michael got it fully stopped.

The kitchen door stood ajar. She screeched, "No!" as she skidded around the corner and faced the sink. Her carefully labeled specimen bottles had disappeared.

Michael came up behind her. "Are we too late?"

Layla's shoulders slumped. "I'm so sorry. I should have taken them with me. I never dreamed they wouldn't be safe in here."

"Looks like nothing around here is safe," Michael said gruffly. "Including us. Do you know how to handle a gun?"

"No. And I don't want to learn. I don't believe in resorting to violence. Guns kill."

"They also protect," he said. "I'm not going to insist, but I would like you to be familiar with firearms. You're a lot better off knowing what *not* to do than you are if you stay ignorant. Think of it as a lesson in personal safety."

Pulling away, Layla walked slowly, pensively, toward the sink where her samples had lain. "I'd much rather rely on Smokey's teeth," she said. "I know he won't make a mistake and bite one of the good guys."

"That's probably true." Michael joined her, turned her to look at him. "Unless the bad guys go after him first. If you won't do it for yourself, do it for Smokey."

Layla scowled and searched his solemn expression. Clearly, he was being earnest. He really did think something might happen to her best four-legged friend.

"All right," she said. "I'll let you teach me. But don't expect Annie Oakley."

"Good. I knew I could count on you."

She huffed in disgust. "I wish that were true. I really let you down when I lost our proof."

Her gaze settled on the contents of the sink. There, in the bottom, lay the scalpel she'd used to obtain her original scrapings. She'd meant to return and properly dispose of the dirty blade but the fire at the barn had distracted her.

Carefully, cautiously, she lifted the scalpel and held it up to the light. There wasn't much residue on the blade but it might be enough, especially since they knew what to test for.

"Bring me one of those clean vials from my bag!" Layla shouted, grinning, "and chalk one up for the good guys. Looks like we've got our answer right here."

Layla sent the sample to a lab in Denver. The results didn't have to be back to convince her she'd made an accurate diagnosis. Just the same, she wanted official confirmation and was relieved when it came.

She and Michael had checked all the other feeders and found nothing amiss. To be on the safe side, she'd recommended that he order fresh grain delivered until his stored feed could be double-checked.

Every time she surveyed the surviving cattle she held her breath. Fortunately, nothing else had gone wrong. As the days passed uneventfully, she began to relax.

Holly found her in the barn with Winona and Wilbur when she dropped in later in the week. "There you are. I've been looking all over for you," Holly said. "Guess I should have known where you'd be."

"Any place but cooped up in the house," Layla replied. "What brings you out this far?"

Holly laughed. "I could say I was just passing by but that's silly. I came to see you." She held out a stiff, white envelope. "Here."

"What is it?" Layla was dusting off her hands.

"Open it and see."

The younger woman's sly expression put Layla on guard. "Why do I get the idea I shouldn't?"

"I haven't a clue." Holly's eyes were twinkling. "Go on. Open it. It won't bite you."

"I'm not so sure." Slowly, deliberately, Layla slipped the engraved card out of the linen-weave envelope and began to read. She was halfway through when she started to shake her head. "Oh, no. Not me. Forget it."

"Don't be a chicken. I'd love to find out I had a secret admirer who was willing to spring for my ticket to a fancy dinner at the Broadmoor."

Layla frowned. "You didn't send this?"

"Hey, not me. I'm just the messenger." She winked. "I guess somebody is trying to talk you into being his valentine."

"No way." Layla thrust the card at her. "I haven't been in town long enough to impress any man this much."

"Maybe one," Holly said with a knowing smirk.

Eyes wide, Layla stared. "No. Not Michael. If he wanted to take me to dinner he'd just ask."

"Would he? I don't know about that. I told you how Tammy broke his heart. Maybe he's playing it safe."

Picturing the luxurious Broadmoor Hotel, Layla continued to resist. "It's ridiculous. Look at me. Do you think I have any clothes suitable for a party like this?"

"That's easy. I do. You can borrow a dress from me."

Layla eyed her up and down. "From you? Thanks, but no thanks. We don't shop at the same kinds of stores."

"So?"

"So, even if you did have a dress that fit me sizewise, which I doubt, it wouldn't suit my style. Besides, I'd feel naked without my jewelry." She fingered one of the silver earrings dangling from her lobes.

"Silver and black go beautifully together," Holly said.

"Black? Ugh. I'd feel like I was going to a funeral." Layla huffed. "My own."

"One night? What can it hurt? Haven't you ever wanted to see the inside of the Broadmoor?"

"Well, sure, but—"

"Then it's settled. The dinner isn't until the evening of the fourteenth so we have plenty of time. Would you like to come to my place and try on clothes or shall I bring a few things out here?"

"I never said I'd go."

"You'll go. I can tell you want to. All you need is a little push."

Making a cynical face, Layla sighed. "A little push? I feel like I've just been run over by a bulldozer!"

Michael open his mail to find a similar invitation. He tossed it aside without even considering attending until his mother phoned.

"Did you pick up your mail today?" Marilyn asked.

"Yeah. Why?"

"Oh, no reason. I thought you might have received an invitation to the Valentine's gala."

"I guess I did."

"So, I'll see you there?"

"Not hardly. I don't have time for parties. There's too much to do here."

"You're working 24/7? You don't fool me, Michael Vance. You're still hiding. It's time you got back into the mainstream. Started living again."

"I'm doing fine as I am, Mom. I don't need any help from you."

"Me? What makes you think I sent you the invitation?"

"Didn't you?"

"As a matter of fact, no," Marilyn said. "I was hoping you'd come to show support for your uncle Max and aunt Lidia. You know how they always participated in Colorado Springs events. This year, I know all your cousins are planning to attend, even if poor Lidia doesn't."

"It means that much to you?"

"Yes," his mother answered soberly. "It means that much to me."

Michael muttered under his breath before he said, "Okay. I'll go. Just don't expect me to stay long."

"Of course not. We wouldn't want anybody to think you were actually enjoying yourself. I can have your father's old tuxedo cleaned and pressed if you want to borrow it."

"Don't push it, Mom. You know how I feel about all that formal posturing. You're lucky I'm going at all, okay?"

"Okay, okay. Forget I suggested it. Love you. Bye."

Michael stared at the receiver as he replaced it. The discarded invitation lay under a pile of papers on his desk. He dug it out. Handling it as if it were fragile—or dangerous—he pulled the card all the way out of the envelope.

There was no indication of who had mailed it. He flipped over the envelope to check for a return address. There was none. However, the invitation had been postmarked in Cripple Creek, not Colorado Springs.

How odd. Puzzled, he stared at the elegant script that spelled out the date and time of the Valentine's Day dinner party. The last time he'd been to the Broadmoor, he'd taken Tammy there to wow her before proposing marriage. He had no desire to be reminded of that night any more than he was looking forward to getting all slicked up to impress a bunch of city folks.

Oh, well. What was done was done. He'd promised. He'd go. At least he'd get a decent meal out of it. The fare Layla had been turning out was so healthy and so devoid of meat he was nearly ready to drive into town just to taste a real burger. Compared to Imelda, the poor woman couldn't cook for beans.

That colloquialism made him chuckle. Vegetables were a big part of the problem. *Beans,* Layla cooked just fine. If he never saw another one it would be too soon.

February fourteenth arrived way too quickly to suit Layla. She and Holly had decided she'd wear a plain black dress with an uneven hem, the most bohemian item in Holly's closet. Since Holly was a couple of inches taller than Layla, the dress fell nearly to the floor. That helped Layla accept its sheer, if drab, drape. Her only complaint was that it wasn't quite long enough to hide her comfortable shoes.

She finally settled on silver sandals she usually wore only in summer. Her toes were freezing but at least she felt she looked halfway presentable. Lacking a dressy coat she donned her down-filled vest and climbed into her truck for the drive down to the Broadmoor. Once she arrived, she could always slip off the vest and leave it in the truck while she made a dash for the door.

Except for a brief incident with a reckless driver,

the entire trip was over before she knew it because she'd been so caught up in retrospection.

How had she let herself be talked into doing this? She didn't belong at the Broadmoor any more than she belonged in the world of the people who frequented it. Her parents had opted out of society by choice. She agreed with their decision. Pretentiousness was to be pitied, not envied.

Rosy lighting of its impressive exterior made the Broadmoor glow like a pink diamond against the starlit sky. As she pulled to a stop under the arched portico she noticed the scrolled letter *B* embedded in mosaic in front of the double doors. It was almost too beautiful to drive over.

A doorman greeted her and a uniformed valet hopped into her truck as soon as she slid from behind the wheel. To her relief and delight, neither man acted as if a pastel-mottled pickup truck was unusual or less than acceptable. When the valet handed her a claim check, she tipped him, hoping she hadn't offered too much or too little. Life on this side of the tracks was a lot more confusing than the simple ways she'd grown up with.

The smiling valet was driving away when she realized she'd forgotten to remove her casual vest. Well, phooey. If the snobs inside didn't like her as she really was, tough.

Squaring her shoulders and tossing her head to throw back her loose curls and display her glittering, dangling earrings and the studs above them, she marched proudly into the lobby.

* * *

Michael Vance was standing near the door to the Broadmoor's largest dining room, Charles Court, talking to a few members of his extended family. When he spied Layla he choked on his ginger ale.

Adam Montgomery clapped him on the back. "I hope you don't need a doctor. This is my night off."

Adam's wife, Kate, was at his side. "Don't worry, honey. Robert Fletcher's here. We can have him or one of the other doctors here Heimlich your brother-in-law if he needs medical attention."

"Very funny." Michael stared at the beautiful blond vision poised in the middle of the foyer. Layla appeared frozen to the spot, like a deer mesmerized in the glare of oncoming headlights.

"Who's that?" Adam asked. "She looks lost."

"That's Layla Dixon, my new vet," Michael said. "No wisecracks, okay? She really is good with animals. She said she already had plans when I asked her to help Norberto and Hector keep an eye on the ranch tonight, but I never dreamed she was coming here."

"Apparently, she was. Aren't you going to go rescue the poor thing?" Kate asked.

Michael scanned the crowd. Spotting neither his mother nor his sister, he sighed. "Guess I should. Except for Mom, Holly and me, Layla doesn't know a soul. I'll go start introducing her before she bolts. Right now, she reminds me of a prairie dog, caught out in the open and being circled by a hungry hawk."

He started away, then turned. "You'd better make

a run for it, too. Here comes Owen Frost. And Yvette Duncan's hot on his trail. Between the deputy mayor and our esteemed councilwoman, that's way too much local politics for me."

Michael left Adam, Kate and several others chuckling behind him as he strode quickly forward to welcome Layla and offer moral support.

The minute Layla spied Michael she was flooded with intense relief. She hadn't wanted to ask her boss if he was planning to attend this party because she didn't want him to think she was making a play for him or hinting she needed a ride. Even if, as Holly had suggested, Michael was her secret admirer, she didn't want to put him on the spot. Seeing him here, however, made her so happy she couldn't stifle her silly grin.

She extended her hand as he neared. "Hello. I didn't know you'd be here."

"I could say the same." Michael gently, briefly, grasped her fingers. His touch was less the handshake of two colleagues than it was the easy greeting of friends who admired each other. "I got drafted by my family. What brings you to the Broadmoor?"

"An anonymous invitation," Layla said. She stared into his dark eyes, hoping to read the truth when she asked, "Do you have any idea who might have sent it?"

"Oh, yes," he said with a smirk. "I have a very good idea where both our invitations came from. Looks like I need to have a long, serious talk with my mother."

"Marilyn? Why her? It was Holly who brought me mine."

"A-ha! The plot thickens."

Layla was glad to see him smiling in spite of their revealing conversation. "We've been had?"

"Sure looks like it."

"I see. What are we going to do about it?"

"That's up to you," Michael said. "Personally, I'd like to strangle them both but I imagine Holly's husband, Jake, would object. See those people over by the door? The good-looking guy with light hair is Jake. I'm seriously outnumbered by his relatives and colleagues at the FBI."

Layla nodded, then reached for his arm and slipped her hand inside the crook of his elbow. "Then I suggest **we** give them what they paid for."

"An excellent idea, ma'am. Unless you're cold, let's check your coat. Then I'll parade you around and introduce you to the gang. They're quite a bunch. Between the Vance and Montgomery families, I'm related to dozens of these characters." He quirked a lopsided grin. "Most of them, I'm even willing to claim."

"Glad to hear it."

He escorted her to the coat check and helped her off with the vest. Though she still felt out of place, Michael's company was quickly banishing her jitters.

"That's an unusual dress," he said. "Is it new?"

"To me, it is." Layla straightened her necklaces and shook her tinkling bracelets to position them optimally. "I borrowed it from your sister. She insisted. At least this way my bright clothes won't embarrass you."

"Embarrass me? Not hardly. If you'll notice, I'm just about the only guy who isn't wearing a tux."

Layla wasn't about to admit she'd noticed immediately. The cut of Michael's dark Western suit set off his athletic build beautifully. So did his cowboy boots. There wasn't a more handsome man in the entire room. Maybe in all of Colorado. That thought made her blush. She lowered her head to hide the reaction.

"We can start by joining Jake and looking for Holly, if you want," Michael suggested. "You probably won't remember everybody's name but I'll be around to cue you if need be."

"Thanks. I'd have better luck if they were animals. I never forget a dog or a cat."

"Or a cow?"

"That, too," Layla said, smiling up at him. "I'm sorry I wasn't available for extra duty tonight."

"No problem. Hector and Norberto are handling it."

"Really? I thought I saw Hector when I first arrived."

Michael's amiable expression faded. "Where?"

Being shorter, Layla had to dodge and stretch to try to catch a second glimpse of the man in question. "Over that way. By the potted fern. I don't know how much you pay your employees but I doubt it's enough to spring for very many parties like this. I shudder to think what a ticket costs."

"Plenty," Michael muttered.

She winced. "Oops. Never mind. The guy just turned around. He doesn't look a bit like Hector from this angle."

Michael visibly relaxed. "I should have known. A ranch foreman would never come to a place like this, even if he could afford the price of admission."

Disappointed, Layla released Michael's arm. "I didn't think you were such a snob."

"I'm not."

"Yes, you are. I suppose you look down on me, too."

"Don't be silly."

She repented enough to offer, "Never mind. Forget it. I need to take my own advice and be less critical, too."

"It's not critical to make an accurate observation," he said. "You have to agree he'd feel out of place."

"Like I do, you mean?"

"I didn't say that."

"I know. Sorry. I wish I looked more elegant, though, like that woman over there. Who is she? I've never seen anyone quite like her."

"That's Dahlia Sainsbury. There is no one like her—at least, not around here. She runs the Impressionist Museum over on Fourth."

"Who's the man she's talking to?" Layla sensed Michael's tension, saw his jaw clench.

"Alessandro." The name was barely audible.

She picked up on his cautionary tone. "Who's Alessandro?"

"Alessandro Donato. A shirttail relative of mine."

"Another relative? So, what else is new?" Layla teased, hoping to lift his spirits. "I gather you don't care for the man."

"Not much. It bothers me every time I see him turning on all that continental charm. Jake and some of the others seem to get along with him well enough. Apparently, I'm averse to bowing and hand kissing."

"Whew! That's a relief." There was mischief in Layla's twinkling blue gaze.

Michael chuckled. "I'm glad you agree." He offered his arm again and placed his warm hand over hers when she obliged. "Shall we go in to dinner, Dr. Dixon?"

"I'd be delighted, Mr. Vance." She stifled a grin and the result was a lopsided smile filled with humor. "I'll trade you my meat course for some of your veggies. Holly tells me the menu is prime rib."

"Deal," Michael said. "Every carrot and pea is yours. I can see we're perfect for each other."

"I wouldn't go that far. But if we're going to hang out all evening to get even with your mother and sister, the least we can do is cater to each other's quirks."

"Eating real food is not a quirk," he countered. "It's a necessity for survival. Why do you think humans have canine teeth?"

"To bite into rutabagas," Layla joked. "Let's go stake our claim to two places side by side before they're all taken and I wind up wasting a good piece of meat."

"I thought you didn't think there was such a thing."

"That was merely a figure of speech," she said, tugging on his arm. "Come on. I'd rather sit over by the picture window, away from the main crowd, if you don't mind."

"Gladly. Too bad we didn't ride down from Cripple Creek together. If we had, we could sneak out early and go home to some peace and quiet."

"I wish I had ridden with you." Her grip tightened. "Parts of SR 67 are really treacherous."

Shepherding her between the red leather-upholstered chairs and elaborately set dining tables he said, "I warned you about that road. Did you have problems?"

"None that were caused by the highway. Some idiot almost ran me into a ditch. I thought I was a goner, for sure." She felt his arm muscles tighten beneath her grasp. "Hey, don't worry. I'm fine."

"You might not have been." Turning, he took both her hands in his. "Did you get a look at the vehicle? Can you identify it?"

"No. It was dark. Everything happened too fast."

"That's what I was afraid of."

"You're not suggesting it was something sinister, are you?"

"I don't know. We seem to be running into more than our share of accidents lately. At least my family does. Since you work for me, I can't help wondering if that means you're included."

Layla sought to allay his fears. "Forget it. I never

stay in one place long enough to get into serious trouble. Besides, who would want to harm an innocent cow mumbler?" She saw a flash of unreadable emotion in his expression before he masked it with a complacent smile.

"Right." Michael pulled out a chair for her before turning to scan the room. "Uh-oh," he said aside. "Brace yourself. Here come the Vances and the Montgomerys. A whole herd of them."

"Is that bad?"

Michael chuckled. "When this night is over, you can tell *me*."

Chapter Six

Conversation at the dinner table was pleasant, if confusing. Layla did her best to follow what was being said, though she was often at a loss. It was perplexing enough having so many different goblets and forks to choose from without also having to keep up a sparkling repartee.

The married couple seated directly across from her, Adam and Kate Montgomery, were proudly celebrating the recent birth of their son, Sean Patrick. Adam was the older brother of Holly's husband, Jake, which made them all kin to Michael. *Big surprise there,* Layla mused.

"So, you're a nurse and Adam's a doctor. Where did you two meet?" she asked Kate. "At work?"

The slightly older woman's amber eyes sparkled. "In a manner of speaking." Kate gave her husband a fond glance and touched his hand. "I didn't know I was in love with the guy until somebody shot him and I thought I might lose him."

Layla nearly dropped her fork. "Shot him? In Colorado Springs?"

"No, no. In the Venezuelan jungle. We were part of a team working with an international volunteer group of medical personnel. A drug-smuggling ring wanted us out of the way, only we didn't know it at the time. It's a long story."

Wide-eyed, Layla looked to Michael. "Don't your family and friends do anything the easy way?"

He grinned. "Nope."

"Hey," Kate said, "I didn't mean to scare you. Everything turned out fine. The FBI and CIA broke up the South American connection, a drug cartel called La Mano Oscura, and Maxwell Vance took care of their Diablo crime syndicate connection back here in the States. All's well that ends well, right?"

Michael's smile faded. "Yeah. Except for what happened to Max."

"Surely that doesn't have any connection to Venezuela," Adam interjected. "Peter assured us that all that nasty business was finished long ago."

Again puzzled, Layla tried to remember if she'd heard Peter's name in the past few hours. "Um, did I meet him?"

"No," Michael replied. "He and Emily decided to stay home after their little boy, Manuel, got the sniffles."

"Speaking of little boys," Kate said. "We can't stay too long. There's nothing crabbier than a hungry baby."

"Or his mother," Adam joked. "Kate takes motherhood very seriously. I almost couldn't get her to come out tonight. To listen to her, you'd think one bottle of formula would ruin Sean Patrick for good."

"It might." His wife gave him a playful whack on the arm. "Besides, if I ever expect to get my figure back, I need to stop stuffing myself." She pushed her gilt-edged plate away and leaned back in the comfortable chair.

Layla approved of Kate's priorities. Any woman who was more concerned about getting home to feed her baby than she was with lingering over elegant cuisine was to be admired.

White-coated waiters had already begun to clear the main course and serve dessert when, two tables away, a tall man with light brown hair and a proud smile stood and tapped his knife against a crystal goblet. A wave of silence radiated like rings of water spreading out from a stone plunked into a still pool. All attention focused on him.

"That's Brendan Montgomery," Michael whispered aside to Layla. "He's Fiona's son."

"The lady who brought us together?"

Michael nodded. "The same. Brendan used to be a Colorado Springs cop. He's with the FBI now."

"That seems to be the career of choice around here."

"It does, doesn't it?" Michael smiled. "Thankfully, I escaped catching the law-enforcement bug. Guess I got my ranching interest from my grandfather, although he was involved in other projects, too."

"Like building the hospital. I know. Holly told me."

Layla couldn't help contrasting her companion's background with her own. The man might seem down-to-earth but his roots were far from commonplace. She was as different from Michael Vance as Smokey was from a prize show dog. Breeding was obviously everything to the close-knit people in this room. And her unconventional family was not one they'd ever approve of.

She saw Brendan hold out his hand to the slim, auburn-haired woman seated beside him and urge her to stand. With a grin, Brendan said, "Most of you know Chloe Tanner from her work at the hospital, especially on behalf of uncle Max." He paused till the murmurs died down. "I was assigned to protect Chloe and her kids, never dreaming the Lord might have more than a short assignment in mind for me."

Layla saw the other woman's cheeks warm and couldn't help smiling in anticipation.

"So," Brendan went on, "we'd like you all to be the first to know. I've asked Chloe to be my wife and she's accepted, with Kyle and Madison's blessings."

A collective cheer and surge of applause went up from the joy-filled room. Quinn Montgomery, one of the men Layla had been introduced to earlier, rose and raised his glass in a toast. "Leave it to Brendan," Quinn boomed. "He not only gets a wonderful wife, he becomes the instant father of two great kids. Here's to my lazy little brother." His grin stretched from ear to ear. "Mom's liable to go broke buying toys!"

One table removed from Quinn, Travis Vance spoke up. "That's right. Tricia and I got our Sofia the hard way. Why should we let Brendan cut corners and jump ahead of us without calling him on it?"

That brought more laughter. Layla joined in the merriment. She knew it was wrong to covet anyone else's happiness, yet she couldn't help being a bit envious of the family moment she was witnessing. That was the crux of her problem, she realized. She was on the outside, looking in, while the others were active participants. They belonged. She never had, even as a child. If she hadn't made the decision to step forward and become a part of God's family at the age of twelve, she didn't know how she'd have coped with being uprooted and placed in a strange community at such an impressionable age.

Was she still searching for the home she felt she'd lost? she wondered. It was a distinct possibility.

Sobering, Layla glanced across at another table where Holly and Jake sat, holding hands and looking at each other with evident affection. Holly's eyes were misty as her husband leaned closer to whisper to her privately. There was so much love in the room, so much joy, Layla's heart wrenched.

She felt, rather than saw, Michael's hand cover hers. When he asked, "Are you okay?" she could only nod.

Marilyn caught up to Layla and Michael as they were leaving. "I see you two found each other," she said with a grin. "How nice." A woman beside her also smiled. Marilyn drew her forward. "Layla, I'd like you to meet Colleen Montgomery, Jake and Adam's sister. She's a reporter at the paper where I work."

Layla politely shook the blue-eyed woman's hand, noting that they were the same height. "Pleased to meet you."

"My pleasure. My parents are here, too," Colleen said. "Frank and Liza. Did you meet them?"

Shaking her head, Layla chuckled softly. "Beats me. I might have. I've met so many Vances and Montgomerys tonight I may *never* straighten them all out."

"Hey, don't worry about it. I'm one of them and *I* sometimes get confused," Colleen quipped.

"I wish they were all blond, like you," Layla told her. "I thought I could tell them apart that way until I met Adam. The gray at his temples makes his dark hair look very distinguished, though."

While Michael stepped aside to speak to Marilyn, Layla stayed with Colleen and perused the crowd leaving the hotel. "Speaking of differences, look at that man coming this way. Michael says he's part of the clan, too."

"Yes and no. His aunt Lidia married into the Vance family when Max was in Italy, so you can't really count Alessandro. Isn't he gorgeous?" Colleen lowered her voice. "I'd like to find out a whole lot more about him than he's willing to let on."

"Sounds more personal than professional."

Colleen's hands fluttered nervously. "Shush. Here

he comes." She smiled and began to blush, much to Layla's amusement.

"Hello, Alessandro," Colleen cooed.

"Cara mia."

When he reached for Colleen's hand and brought it languidly to his lips, Layla made sure hers were tucked safely behind her. She would have retreated to Michael's side if she hadn't been worried about making a social faux pas that would embarrass everyone.

"And who is your beautiful companion?" Alessandro asked with a voice as smooth as warm caramel on a summer day.

"This is Layla Dixon. She works for Michael on the Double V."

"Ah, surely not," he said.

To Layla's relief he'd continued to hold Colleen's hand rather than reach for hers.

"What do you do, lovely lady?" He winked at Layla. "Or is it gauche of me to ask?"

Layla squared her shoulders and lifted her chin. "I'm a veterinarian, and a good one, in case you were wondering that, too."

Alessandro gave a slight bow. "Forgive me, Doctor. I meant no offense." He again caressed the backs of Colleen's fingers with his lips, said, "Until we meet again," and strode away as if he owned the hotel and everything in it.

Layla blinked. "Wow."

Sighing, Colleen gave a dreamy nod. "Tell me about it. One look from that guy can toast the socks right off my feet. Whatever you do, don't tell my mother. She's already driving me crazy about being single, especially now that my brothers have settled down. If she had her way, she'd have me committed to a new blind date every weekend."

"My mom's the opposite," Layla said. "She couldn't care less what I do or don't do. My dad, either. Which reminds me. I ought to give them a call one of these days, tell them where I am."

Colleen's eyes widened. "They don't know?"

"No. I've been on my own for a long time. They never complain as long as I check in once in a while."

"Whew! I don't know which is worse, feeling like I have my folks in my pocket every second or being isolated, like you are."

"I travel with a dog. I'm never lonesome."

"Don't you miss talking to people?"

At that moment, Michael stepped back into their conversation with a smile. "Layla doesn't miss a thing. She talks to animals. You should have seen her with that heifer I bought at the fair last year. She mumbled in that cow's ear and it acted like she was giving it a Lamaze lesson."

Layla shot him a quirky smile. "It worked, didn't it?"

"It certainly did." He placed his hand gently at her elbow as he said, "We have a long drive home. We'd better be going."

Marilyn immediately brightened. "You rode together? I thought—"

"No, Mom. We drove separately," Michael said.

"But I'm going to follow Dr. Dixon so I can look out for her."

Colleen and Marilyn asked, "Why?" in unison.

"It's dark and the roads may be icy," Michael answered. He gave Layla a silent signal with his eyes to hold her peace. "It's best to be careful, don't you think?"

"Absolutely." Layla smiled at the women. "Nice to see you again, Mrs. Vance. And nice meeting you, Colleen."

Michael spoke earnestly. "I saw you two talking to Alessandro just now. Watch yourselves around him."

Layla could see that Colleen wasn't pleased to be receiving such personal advice, particularly from Michael, so she took the initiative before the other woman could speak up.

"Let's go grab my vest before the line out there gets any longer." With her back to Michael, she waggled her eyebrows at Colleen. "Good luck with everything."

Michael followed Layla to the coat-check room and handed in their claim checks.

"You're not really going to follow me home, are you?" she asked.

"I certainly am."

As soon as her vest arrived, she snatched it before he could offer to help her put it on. "If I'd thought for one minute you'd overreact like this, I'd never have mentioned the reckless driver."

"Why not?"

"Because I don't need a babysitter. I'm all grown up. I can take care of myself."

"Glad to hear it. What's your point?"

She paused at the door and faced him, hands fisted on her hips. "What's my point? I just told you. I don't need your help."

"Okay," he drawled, "then let's say I need yours. I'd hate to see you get killed before I was through picking your brain. You *are* the only one who's made any headway figuring out the cause of my losses."

"I hadn't looked at it quite that way."

"Well, start," he said flatly. "If I was concerned about Norberto or Imelda, or even Hector, I'd do the same thing for them. When I hired you, you became my responsibility."

"Just like one of your cattle."

"Exactly."

Layla wasn't sure she liked the analogy but she had to admit the man had a valid point. While they were working at the Double V, they were all a team. And Michael Vance was their team leader. Therefore, unlike his inappropriate advice to Colleen, he was entitled to proprietary concern in her regard no matter how much it grated.

"Okay. Follow me if you want," she said. "Just don't try to tell me how to drive, okay?"

His laugh was mocking. "Perish the thought."

Michael had little trouble following Layla's unusual truck. He easily kept her in sight while they were on the main highway. When they turned off toward Cripple Creek on SR 67, he was second in line behind her. That was good enough. He didn't figure anybody would try anything funny when there were witnesses.

The winding, two-lane road had to climb from the six-thousand-foot altitude of Colorado Springs to nearly eight thousand feet before it reached the turnoff to the Double V. That was still fifteen hundred feet shy of Cripple Creek's official 9,508 foot elevation.

The dark sedan between Michael and Layla slowed and signaled to turn onto one of the many gravel side roads they were passing. Michael braked. Layla's truck was rapidly pulling away but he wasn't worried. Nobody was going to pass him. Not if he had anything to say about it.

He drummed his fingers on the steering wheel and muttered at the slow driver. "Come on. Turn it. You can do it. Atta boy. Good for you. Now goose it."

As soon as he knew his front bumper would clear the other car, Michael floored the gas pedal. The pickup's engine roared. Gripping the wheel, he squinted into the darkness. Curves in the road ahead were keeping him from spotting the glow from Layla's taillights but he knew she was still there. All he had to do was catch up.

Rounding a particularly nasty corner, Michael saw a flicker of red. He was about to heave a sigh of relief when he noted that there were *two* sets of taillights. While he'd been delayed, another car had apparently pulled out from one of the myriad side roads and there was once again a third vehicle in their convoy.

That shouldn't have bothered him but it did. The toe of his boot pushed harder on the gas. The truck shuddered, slewed on the slick roadway, then straightened out. Michael's heart was in his throat. He knew he was driving like a madman, yet something kept spurring him on, insisting he must stay close to Layla.

"I'm a fool," he told himself. "I won't do anybody any good if I wreck, least of all, myself."

That logical conclusion should have been enough to convince him to slow down to a sensible speed. It wasn't.

Layla hadn't been able to tell exactly who was behind her for miles. Michael's truck was black, so that was no help at all. Except for the way pickup lights rode higher above the ground, especially on four-wheel-drive vehicles, they all looked the same in her rearview mirror.

A few miles back she'd noticed that there were no headlights following and had considered pulling off the road to wait for Michael to catch up. Then, suddenly, there he was, bearing down on her again.

She smiled in relief. She'd never admit it, of course, but it was a comfort to know he was looking out for her. This road could be a white-knuckler. She planned to avoid driving it at night in the future, particularly when there was snow and ice to contend with. Like now.

They were probably less than halfway home and her fingers were already cramped from grasping the steering wheel too tightly. There were times, particularly in the summer when she could comfortably travel with the windows open, that she enjoyed driving. This was *not* one of those times.

Layla yawned. Being too warm always made her sleepy. If her toes hadn't been freezing in the silver strapped sandals she wouldn't have turned the heater on in the first place. To give herself a jolt of fresh, cold air she rolled the driver's side window partway down and took invigorating breaths. *There. That was better.*

The headlights behind her flashed, moved slightly left. It looked as if the other vehicle was jockeying to pass! What was wrong with Michael? Had he lost his mind?

Easing as far as she could to the right shoulder, Layla felt her tires bump over rocks and ice on the berm. She braked, started to slide, fishtailed when she straightened the wheel, fought to maintain control.

The other truck pulled parallel. With a quick glance, Layla shouted, "Michael, you idiot!" before she realized that the driver was *not* her concerned boss.

This man was wearing a ski mask! He whipped ahead of her. Cut her off. Clipped her bumper. Forced her farther off the road.

Layla tried in vain to hold her place. Her truck was too lightweight in comparison to that of her assailant. Even four-wheel drive wasn't enough to save her.

Her right fender slid along a low metal railing edging the road. With a shower of sparks and a squealing grind, she bounced back against her attacker's vehicle, then overcorrected.

That was a critical mistake. In an instant she was through the rail and airborne, screaming and plummeting over the edge of the narrow mountain road!

All she could think of on the way down was how mad Michael was going to be and how thankful she was that Smokey wasn't with her this time.

Watching the incident take place and the other truck speed away, Michael felt totally helpless.

He raced to the scene, skidded to a stop and leaped from his truck shouting, "Layla!" There was no answer.

With his headlights to guide him, he ran through the break in the railing and over the edge of the icy ravine. A copse of trees had caught Layla's truck a short way down and stopped her death-defying plunge.

It was impossible for Michael to tell what lay beyond her precarious perch. He didn't hesitate. Slipping and sliding his way through the thick, broken vegetation, he yanked on the driver's door till he got it open.

"Layla?"

Her moan of response tied his gut in knots. He reached across to turn off the ignition, then unfastened her taut seat belt. The truck was too old to have air bags but the belt had kept her from flying into the shattered windshield.

Gently, tenderly, he brushed her hair off her forehead. She didn't stir. He knew it was unwise to move her so *now* what? Like an idiot he'd left his cell phone in his truck. If he climbed back to the road to get it and call for help, Layla might come to, struggle out of the wreck by herself, and make matters worse. Groggy, she might even fall the rest of the way to the valley floor!

Michael's breath caught. *Gasoline fumes!* The old pickup was leaking fuel.

"Lord, help me. I can't leave her like this. Not now." Taking as much care as he could under the challenging circumstances, he eased her out and into his arms, then turned and started to carry her back up to the highway.

Chapter Seven

Half off, half on the road, Michael's empty, still-running truck had rapidly gathered a small crowd of bystanders.

Layla's head lay on his shoulder. She'd come to her senses enough to place a hand against his chest and had stopped moaning, although he still wasn't sure how badly she might be hurt.

"Somebody call 911," Michael ordered as strong hands reached to help him climb the last few yards to the highway.

"Already did," a stranger answered. "What happened?"

"Some idiot crowded her off the road." Michael opened the passenger door of his truck and gently placed Layla on the seat, releasing her reluctantly.

She blinked, looked up at him and winced, trembling. "Boy, am I glad to see you."

"Are you okay?"

"I think so. How's my poor truck?"

"It's seen better days," he said honestly. "What happened? I saw a crazy driver trying to pass on a curve. The next thing I knew, you were airborne."

Layla's shivering increased. Michael slung his much larger leather coat around her shoulders and gently drew it together in the front like a blanket.

She licked her lips. Tears misted her eyes. "He hit me on purpose. Twice. I tried to fight back, to keep my wheels on the road. But he got me to sliding and over I went."

Michael's arm encircled her. He pulled her close, held her tenderly. When Layla buried her face against his shoulder and began to cry quietly he thought his heart would burst. Part of him wanted to speed off after the attacker and beat him to a pulp. A more rational side of him wanted nothing more than to stand there beside this weeping woman and comfort her as long as she'd let him.

Rationality won out. So did tenderness. Without conscious thought, Michael bent and placed a kiss on Layla's hair.

She lifted her face to smile at him through her tears, as if she, too, wanted the moment to last.

Red lights and sirens were approaching from below. One of the passersby flagged down the rescue truck and ambulance.

Paramedics took over and gave Layla a cursory examination while Michael hovered nearby, talking to the police. He heard Layla say, "No. I don't want to go to the hospital. I'm feeling fine. Really," before he stepped forward to take charge.

"I can drive her home," Michael said. "She lives at the Double V ranch, closer to Cripple Creek. I'll keep an eye on her. If she starts to feel worse, I'll see she gets to a doctor up there right away."

Layla grimaced. "Can't I drive my truck?"

"I doubt that very much," he answered. "Even if it'll start after it's pulled back onto the road, I think you have a ruptured fuel line. We can probably fix that at the ranch." He smiled. "Besides, you're in no shape to be driving."

"Who says?"

"I do." He gave her a lopsided grin. "In case you haven't noticed, you're doing a great imitation of an aspen."

Layla held out her hands and looked at them. "Quaking?"

"Quaking. Now, what do you need out of your truck before we go? Did you have a purse or anything like that?"

"Nope. Pockets," she said, patting the sides of her vest. "I'm good to go as soon as I sign the release for the ambulance guys." One of them thrust a clipboard at her and she scrawled her signature where he indicated.

Michael hadn't left her side. "Okay. Wait here. I'll go tell the police to have your truck towed to the ranch."

"Won't they need to take a report? Ask me questions?"

"They said that can wait. You didn't recognize the other driver, right?"

"Right." She made a face.

"Then don't worry about it. I'll speak to my cousin Sam and have him handle the details for us."

"Sam Vance? The homicide detective I heard about tonight? Why *him?*"

Michael's nostrils flared in anger. "Because this was no accident, Layla."

She shivered from head to toe. "Maybe the guy left paint scrapes on my truck that can be traced. He hit me hard enough."

"The cops can check for that when they haul your truck out of the gulley."

After he'd explained to the officers, he thanked the rescuers and private citizens who had stopped to help, then returned to his truck and slid behind the wheel. "Ready?"

Layla's arms were folded tightly across her chest. "Ready."

"Fasten your seat belt. It saved your life once tonight."

"That was a close one, wasn't it?"

"Too close. Here. Lay my jacket over your legs like a blanket. It'll keep you warmer. Don't you have a regular coat? One with sleeves?"

"This vest had detachable sleeves. Smokey chewed them up when I first got him." She was straining to fasten the safety belt. Michael reached to help. She let him. "Thanks. I guess I am a little sore and shaky."

"I suspect you'll be more than a little sore by tomorrow," he said soberly. "Remember, if you start to feel sick or act strange, I'm taking you straight to a doctor."

"Oh, yeah? I've never been anything *but* strange. How in the world will you be able to tell if I'm acting funnier than usual?"

He placed his hand over hers where it rested on the seat. "Believe it or not, I'm used to your ways. I'll know." He felt her tremble beneath his touch.

"Thanks. For everything," Layla said. "I hate to think what might have happened if you hadn't been following me."

"So do I."

Michael's mind raced as he drove the familiar road. Layla's first so-called accident might have been overlooked. The second removed all doubt. Even if she hadn't been certain that this driver was bent on forcing her off the precipitous road, he'd have suspected foul play. First his innocent cattle and now this.

Michael's jaw muscles clenched. Maybe the cattle weren't the first victims. Ben was still unaccounted for. If his missing foreman wasn't guilty of negligence or purposeful poisoning of the stock, maybe he, too, was a casualty of whoever or whatever was behind all these catastrophes. It was easier to believe that than it was to accept the idea that Ben had reverted to his old ways and was somehow taking it out on the Double V.

Michael's jaw clenched. Now, Layla Dixon was

apparently involved right up to her pretty neck, too. Was it too late to send her away for her own good? Probably. Anyone who'd try to harm her when there was a good chance of being seen or even captured, like tonight, had to be desperate enough to track her no matter where she went.

Given those facts, Michael decided the safest place for Layla was right where she was. Beside him. The closer the better.

He wasn't sure how he was going to handle the situation once they reached the Double V but he wasn't going to leave her alone until he was certain she hadn't suffered a head injury. All he'd have to do was convince her his intentions were honorable, which they were, and decide how he was going to remain nearby without compromising her reputation.

He glanced over at her, found she'd closed her eyes, and reacted immediately. "Hey, Doc. Wake up. You're not supposed to sleep."

Layla yawned. "Oh, yeah? Tell that to my eyelids. They're unbelievably heavy."

"Maybe you have a concussion."

She shook her head. "No way. Nothing hurts up there and my vision is fine. I'm a doctor, remember?"

"An animal doctor. That doesn't count."

"Oh yeah? Well, let me tell you something, Michael Vance, the schooling for MDs and vets is essentially the same. The only difference is, we can't ask our patients what hurts or how they feel. The way I look at it, we have to be better doctors than the ones who treat humans."

He grimaced. "I suppose that means you don't intend to take any advice from me."

"Of course not." Layla yawned. "To tell you the truth, I think I'd be just as tired whether my truck had landed in a ditch or not. Being in that crowd at the hotel took a lot out of me. I'm not used to so much socializing."

"Neither am I." He snorted derisively and shook his head. "Give me a horse and the open range any time."

"Speaking of horses, I've been meaning to ask if I could go riding sometime. When I was growing up at the commune, my best friends were horses. I missed them the most when my folks moved back to the city."

"Of course you can ride. You should have asked sooner."

"I didn't want to be a pest." Laying her head back against the seat she sighed and smiled slightly. "I did explore the barns and find where you keep the horses, though. They're beautiful. Especially the Arab-looking gray mare. What's she crossed with? Mustang?"

"Yes," Michael said. "You have quite an eye. What else did you notice?"

"That your stock is well kept and healthy. The big Appaloosa gelding is magnificent, too. He's in prime condition even though he's got some years on him. What's his name?"

"You're going to love it. I call him, the Appaloosa."

"How original."

"I'm almost afraid to ask. What have you named him?"

"How about *Spot?*" Layla stifled a giggle. "Just kidding. I hadn't thought about giving him a name until now. I was positive he'd already have one."

"Even if he did," Michael countered, "you'd still have called him something else."

"Probably." She yawned again, covering her mouth with her hand. "Sorry. I really am beat."

Michael figured he wouldn't have a better opportunity to address his concerns for her health so he plunged ahead. "I think I should keep an eye on you for a few more hours. Just to make sure you're not going to conk out."

"I never conk," Layla said. "I am looking forward to a sleep, though. Trust me. You don't have to sit up with me. I'm fine."

"Still—"

"No. It's not open to discussion. Drop me at the cabin and go home."

"Just like that?"

Layla gave him a determined look when she said, "Yes. Just like that."

Morning found Layla achy and stiff. She kneaded the back of her neck with one hand and rotated her head to try to relieve the kinks. One shoulder was striped with a two-inch-wide bruise caused by the upper portion of the seat belt. Other than that, she hadn't found any visible injuries. Truth to tell, the whole incident seemed like a bad dream.

Except for the part where Michael had kissed the top of her head and held her so lovingly, she countered, smiling. That was definitely no nightmare. Who'd have guessed that the crusty rancher had such a tender side?

"I would have," she answered. A person only had to watch him with livestock to see that he was a kind man. In spite of his uncompromising attitude, he cared. Deeply. He couldn't help it that he'd been raised in such a stuffy, conventional family, any more than she could help her upbringing. It was simply a fact of life.

Living at the commune, she'd felt a part of society. That had changed once her parents had moved to the city. Other children had laughed at her, taunted her for her unusual clothing and natural ways. Oh, she'd learned how to fit in, at least on the outside. In her heart, however, she'd remained an outcast. And she still was.

Layla was dressed and almost ready to head for the ranch house. She stopped at the mirror in the bathroom to brush her hair. Smokey was at her heels. This time however, instead of tagging along behind as he usually did, he forged ahead. Using his body to nudge her toward the door, he bristled and began to growl.

Hesitating, Layla frowned. "What is it, boy? What's the matter?"

The dog was concentrating on a small, secluded area between the commode and the sink cabinet. Layla edged closer. Peered into the dark corner.

At first she thought she was seeing a crumpled bath towel. Then, the object moved!

Smokey jumped, startled. Layla caught his collar to keep him from lunging. Something was slowly rising from the pile. An arrow-shaped head, colored in diamonds of varying brown tones, pointed directly at her. The eyes were yellow, pupils barely slits. The forked tongue darted out, waving in exploration and assessment.

Layla could hardly move, hardly breathe. Before her brain had fully identified the creature as a rattlesnake, instinct had insisted she flee. Only her fear for Smokey's safety kept her from screaming and running. If she let go of the fiercely protective dog, he'd surely attack the snake in her defense and be bitten!

Every muscle tense, she backed slowly toward the door, tugging Smokey with her. He resisted, his claws scratching the slick floor. If Layla's grip hadn't been augmented by surging adrenaline, she might not have had the strength to restrain him.

Yellow eyes tracked their progress. Behind the coiled body a tail vibrated with the characteristic warning of a timber rattler.

Layla felt the rug beneath her feet. They were in the clear! Still holding tight to her faithful dog, she caught hold of the doorknob in her free hand and slammed the door shut, trapping the snake in the bathroom.

Were they safe now? It sure didn't feel like it. Whirling, she dragged Smokey with her to the outside door and burst onto the porch without looking. All she cared about was getting away from danger. Fast!

Michael had been about to knock. Layla careened

into him at a run. In her frenzied state, she cut loose with a scream that echoed through the quiet mountain valley like a siren.

Michael staggered and caught her, righting them both. "Whoa! What's wrong?"

Layla pointed mutely. Smokey was pawing at the now-closed door, trying desperately to get back into the cabin.

"S-s-snake."

"Where?"

"Bathroom." She grabbed his arm as he reached for the door. "No! Don't go in there. It's really big."

Shaking his head as if he thought she was imagining things, Michael said, "That's impossible. This is the middle of winter. All the snakes are hibernating."

"Not *that* one."

He hesitated, studying her expression. "I can see you've had a scare. Trust me, it can't be a snake."

"Oh, yeah?" Layla was getting perturbed. "Listen, cowboy, you may think you know all about snakes but I'm no novice, either." She gestured wildly toward the cabin. "*That* is a rattlesnake. If Smokey hadn't warned me, you'd be hauling me to the hospital right now. Or worse."

"Okay. I'll take it slow. Stay here. As soon as I've looked the place over and made sure there's no danger, I'll call you."

"Yeah, right." She released his arm and took hold of her dog's collar. "Okay. Go look. But watch your step. I shut the thing in the bathroom. Unless it slithered under the door it should still be there."

The look Michael gave her was one of tolerance laced with disbelief. Nevertheless, he was cautious when he opened the door and entered the cabin.

Listening as best she could over Smokey's rumbling growl, Layla could hear Michael's footsteps progressing. She envisioned him stopping at the bathroom and easing open the door. His colorful exclamation removed all doubt that he'd found her unwelcome visitor.

There was a rustling. A thump. Another mumbled comment she was glad she couldn't fully hear.

Time seemed to creep by. Layla was about to peek inside when Michael reappeared, carrying a pillowcase with a lump the size of a throw pillow in the bottom. Arm extended, he carefully walked past her.

"You caught it?"

"Yes. Wait for me. I'll be right back."

Layla sagged against the wall, then slid to a seat on the floor of the porch. She felt as if she'd just run a marathon. Smokey lay beside her and rested his head on her lap. Clearly, he was certain the threat had passed.

To her dismay, tears threatened. She felt like a ninny. There was no reason to cry. All was well. Michael had come to the rescue and nothing bad had happened. Maybe that was what bothered her. She wasn't used to relying on anyone but herself and it galled her to have to keep leaning on Michael.

He returned quickly.

"What did you do with it?" Layla asked.

"What any rancher would do. It wouldn't have survived in this weather, anyway. What I can't figure out is why it was awake. Maybe it was hibernating in the cabin all along and the warmth of your fires woke it up."

"Oh, that's comforting," she said wryly. "Do you think it had friends?"

"Not likely."

Layla knew different. Snakes tended to congregate. If that one was in her cabin by accident, there was a good chance he wasn't sleeping alone. She raised an eyebrow at the stoic rancher. Since Michael wasn't worried about other snakes in the immediate vicinity, chances were he'd decided the rattler had been placed in her cabin to frighten her. *She* certainly thought so.

When he held out his hand, she took it and let him help her up. "I'm glad you showed up this morning. What brought you down here?" Layla was dusting off her jeans.

"I wanted to see how you were feeling."

"Pretty good, considering."

"I also came to get you so you wouldn't have to walk to the house. Are you ready to go?"

"More than ready."

She wasn't particularly keen on cooking, especially after all that had just happened, but she wasn't the type to shirk duty. And she certainly wasn't ready to reenter her cabin. Not yet.

He escorted her to the waiting truck. "How are you really feeling? Be honest."

"Achy. Grumpy. Sore. Shaky. Pick one."

"Sounds like it's all of the above. Don't worry. You can have the day off. I decided to make coffee and hard-boil some eggs this morning. I figured I could manage that much."

"Wow. I'm impressed."

"Yeah. Me, too," he said with a chuckle. "Now that I know I can boil water without burning it, there's no telling what else I can fix."

"Could I have hot tea?" Layla asked. "That's another boiling water thing, so it should be within your scope of expertise."

"I think I can manage. You didn't even have to teach me how to light the burners on the stove."

"You are a quick study, aren't you?"

"I try." He sobered. "There are a few things that have slipped under my radar, though. I've been doing a lot of thinking, especially since last night. This morning's excitement only confirms my decision."

"Uh-oh. Am I fired?"

"No way." He brought the truck to a stop behind the ranch house and turned to face her instead of getting out right away. "On the contrary. I think you and I should stick closer than we have been. If I'm working outside, that's where I want you to be. If you have to start cooking or something, I'll come inside."

"Why?"

"I don't want you to be alone."

"Why not? What did I do?"

"Almost got yourself killed, for starters."

"Hey, I couldn't help that."

"I know. While you're here, your life may be in danger. Until we figure out what's been going on, I aim to be your shadow. Period. End of discussion."

"End of discussion, nothing. I'm not one of your cows. You can't stick me in a corral and keep me prisoner just so you don't have to worry about me."

Michael snorted derisively. "I wish it was that simple. I never dreamed you were going to fight me over this."

Layla sighed, then looked at him sadly. "Maybe I should just go."

"Is that what you want to do?"

"No, but—"

"Then don't even consider it. Think for a minute. It won't be so bad. You like working outdoors and I could use a few survival tips in the kitchen." He glanced at the house. "Besides, you hate housecleaning."

"How can you tell?"

"Trust me. I can tell," he said. The corners of his mouth were twitching. "You've never even asked me where we keep the vacuum cleaner."

"I didn't need to know."

"Exactly. So, is it a deal? Are we partners till we figure out the puzzle?" He seemed relieved when she mirrored his expression.

"Okay," she said. "But absolutely *no* roping or branding."

"We don't brand cattle anymore. We use ear tags."

Layla giggled and fingered a dangling earring. "Not the cows, silly. I meant *me*."

Layla and Michael were still in the kitchen when Sam Vance arrived and let himself in with a cheery, "Morning."

Michael stood and greeted him. "Sam! Good to see you. Sam Vance, I'd like you to meet Layla Dixon. Have they pulled her truck out yet?"

"Ma'am." Sam nodded to accentuate the greeting, then answered. "Yes. There was paint from the other vehicle on the damaged fender, like you thought. We'll send samples to be tested."

"Is my truck here?" she asked. "I want to go see it."

"We'll all go," Michael said.

Sam gave him a cautious look and held up his hand. "Dr. Dixon can go by herself. Detective Hilliard rode with me. She's waiting outside."

Though he didn't like being separated from her, Michael capitulated. "Okay. We'll join you in a sec."

As soon as Layla had left, Michael faced his cousin. "All right. What else?"

"Got a cup of coffee?"

"Sure." Michael poured a mug for Sam and refilled his own. "Here's your coffee. Talk."

"How much do you know about your lady friend?"

"She used to live around here, over by Manitou Springs, and she's a licensed veterinarian. Why?"

"Is that all?"

"Pretty much." Michael was scowling. "Why all these questions about Layla? She was the victim last night, not the one responsible for the crash."

Sam took a slow sip from his mug. "So you said. Where did she go after you rescued her?"

"Nowhere. We came straight back here and I dropped her at the cabin."

"The one Holly and Jake stayed in when they were on the run from the drug cartel?"

"The same. What are you getting at? Spit it out."

"Didn't it strike you as odd that I'd show up to take this report myself?"

Michael shrugged. "Not really. You're family. I asked you to handle it for Layla's sake. I wanted to get her away from the scene last night and the easiest way to do that was to give the officers your name. Anyway, as far as I'm concerned, her accident was an attempted homicide, right up your alley."

"It may be more complicated than that," Sam said. "Early this morning, I got a call there was a body found in a truck near the airport. It looked like suicide by carbon monoxide." He paused, scowled. "I bought that cause of death until I noticed fresh purple and pink scrape marks on the right front fender and bumper of the deceased's vehicle."

"From Layla's truck?"

"I'd say there's a high probability," Sam told him.

Astonished, Michael stared, unseeing, at the door she'd recently passed through. "Who was the guy? Do you know?"

"Yeah. Harry Redding, a petty crook we've had our eye on for years. Worked for Ritchie Stark, a guy with a rap sheet as long as my arm. Good old Ritchie has an alibi for last night or he'd be at the top of my suspect list."

"This is unbelievable."

Sam snorted. "It gets better. Chloe already

thought Redding was the man she surprised in the hospital when he was trying to finish off Dad."

"Whoa. I thought Brendan had had that sleazeball arrested and carted off to jail after he collared him at Chloe's house."

"He did. Redding got a sharp lawyer and made bail."

Scowling, Michael grabbed Sam's arm so roughly his coffee sloshed. "Are you telling me this whole thing is tied together? The dead guy is the one who shot Max, attacked Chloe at the hospital and just tried to kill Layla?"

"It's starting to look like it."

"Does that mean it's all over? Max is safe now?"

Sam shook his head. "We're not taking the guards off Dad's hospital room door, if that's what you're asking. Assuming Redding was murdered rather than committing suicide, we know there has to be at least one more person involved. If I were a betting man, which I'm not, I'd wager the circle is much more extensive."

"Why us?" Michael was beside himself.

"I don't know." Sam spoke slowly, pensively. "But I do know that we'd all better keep our eyes open. I have a feeling this vendetta, or whatever it is, is a lot bigger than any of us have dared imagine."

Chapter Eight

Layla chatted with the driver of the tow truck and a friendly woman detective who had introduced herself as Rebecca Hilliard, Becca for short. When Michael and his cousin joined them outside, Becca busied herself taking paint scrapings and checking out the damage to the truck rather than take an active part in Sam's discussion.

Michael looked awful. Layla could only guess what was upsetting him because, like every man she'd ever known, he was being closemouthed. Well, fine. Let him brood. If he didn't want to help her look into getting her poor, beat-up truck repaired, she'd see to it herself. And if her continued presence was making him too uptight, she'd pack her bags and hit the road again—as soon as she had wheels.

Scanning the damage to her trusty vehicle, she sighed. There was clearly more wrong with the dear old thing than a simple dented fender. She was bending down, peering at the undercarriage, when Sam approached.

"How's it look?" he asked.

"Not good." Layla straightened. "I don't think she was pigeon-toed before. I'm afraid the axle may be broken."

"Well, you did land in a tree. Sort of." He gave her a friendly smile. "I think you'd better have the radiator checked, too."

That reminded her of the poisoned cattle. "Oh, no! It isn't leaking, is it?"

"Not anymore," Sam said. "It's empty."

"What about the wild animals? If they lap it up…"

Sam raised his hand in a gesture of calm. "Don't worry. The tow truck took care of any spills."

"Michael said it was leaking gas, too. He was afraid it was going to catch fire."

"Not once the engine cooled down." Reaching into the breast pocket of his jacket, Sam pulled out a small piece of paper. "Mike tells me you used to live around here."

"A long time ago, when I was a kid. Why?"

"Just curious." He displayed a photo. "Does this guy look familiar?"

"I don't think so." Layla shaded her eyes with her hand and studied the grainy picture more closely, trying to jog her memory. "No, I'm afraid not. Who is he?"

"His name is Redding, but at last count he was going by six or seven different aliases. Look closely at his face. He has a spider tattoo on his left wrist. You sure you haven't seen him? Maybe years ago?"

"I was twelve when we moved away, Detective." Layla looked to Michael. "What's going on here? Am I supposed to recognize this man?"

Michael took his place at her side, as protective as he'd been right after the accident. "No. You're not. The police are just following up on a few leads, aren't you, Sam?"

"Gotta check 'em all," he said as he stuck the photo back into his pocket. "Well, take care. I hope your truck isn't totaled."

"So do I," Layla replied. "I can't hit the road without a decent set of wheels."

Sam paused. "If I were you, I wouldn't plan on going anywhere for a while, Dr. Dixon." He nodded toward his female partner. "Detective Hilliard or I may need to talk to you again."

Layla felt Michael's hand lightly at her elbow, as if he were shielding her. But from what? She certainly didn't need protection from the police. They were all on the same side of the law.

Michael's expression was shadowed by the brim of his Stetson, emphasizing his determination with perhaps a hint of anger. Maybe even a little alarm. That was the most disquieting. She and the rugged rancher had already been through plenty of trauma together and he'd never shown the slightest weakness. If, now, he felt he had reason to be afraid of someone or something, she knew the situation was worse than she'd imagined.

The tow truck departed. Becca stopped to shake Layla's hand and present a business card. "If you think of anything else that might help, please give me a call."

"I will," Layla said. "Thanks." She watched the amiable officer get into the unmarked police car.

Sam paused by the driver's door and addressed Michael. "See you in church tonight?"

He shrugged. "With all that's happened, I forgot. This is Sunday, isn't it?"

"All day. I had to work but I'll be off duty later. Jessi took Amy to Sunday School this morning. She really looks forward to going."

"Sorry, Sam. I should have asked about your family. How are the twins?"

"Fat, sassy and beginning to sleep longer," he said proudly. "I may live through their early years after all." Waving, he slid behind the wheel of the car, slammed the door and drove away.

Layla turned to face Michael, her hands fisted on her hips. "Okay, mister. What's going on? And who is that weasel-faced guy in the picture?"

"A petty criminal."

"Then why did Sam seem so sure I'd know him? I've never even gotten a parking ticket." She arched an eyebrow. "Not since I got out of college, anyway."

"Redding was found in a truck with pink and purple scrapes along the side. Sam's pretty sure he was the one who ran you off the road."

"Well, why didn't somebody say so?" Layla wrapped her arms around herself and shivered. "I wish I'd taken a better look at the photo, tried to memorize the guy's face. I want to recognize him in case I run into him again—figuratively speaking."

"You won't," Michael said flatly.

"Oh, sure. That's easy for you to say. He didn't do his best to send you to kingdom come."

Gently, cautiously, Michael cupped his hands around the points of her shoulders and faced her. "I know he won't try to hurt you again."

She tried to twist away but he held her fast. "How can you be so positive?"

"Because he was found dead this morning. In the same truck that was used to try to kill you."

Layla gasped. "What—what did he die of?"

"Carbon monoxide. Sam said it looked like a suicide."

"But?" She could tell Michael was holding back a lot more than he was revealing. "Come on. Tell me. I have a right to know."

"Sam suspects Redding may have been murdered. At least he's investigating his death that way until he can prove otherwise."

"And if he can't?" Layla didn't want to know more, yet she had to ask. Staying naive while the world around her was coming unraveled was more than foolish. It was dangerous.

"If it turns out Redding didn't commit suicide," Michael said soberly, "then we'll know for sure that others were involved."

Layla shivered. When Michael opened his arms, she stepped into his embrace without hesitation and laid her cheek on his chest. "This is getting scary."

To her chagrin, Michael agreed. "Yes. It is. I wish I could do more to protect you."

"I'll settle for a hug like this once in a while," Layla joked, trying to keep from taking his comforting nearness too seriously. She backed slowly away and smiled up at him. "Thanks. I needed that."

Michael looked relieved and a little embarrassed. He touched the brim of his hat and nodded as he said, "My pleasure, ma'am."

Late that afternoon, having checked every nook and cranny for venomous creatures and finding none, Layla was pacing the cabin floor and trying to accept Michael's revelation. She'd relived the incident so many times, the details of running off the road were beginning to blur.

When she closed her eyes she could visualize the attacker looking back at her from his speeding truck, but what good was that memory when he'd been wearing a ski mask? It could have been anyone. It still might be. There was no ironclad guarantee that the man who had died in the damaged truck was working alone. Maybe he wasn't even the person who had smashed it into her!

She hoped the dead man had been her attacker. To believe otherwise left too many loose ends.

Michael's knock on her door startled her. She managed a smile just the same. "Hi."

"Hello, sunshine."

"It's Rainbow," Layla said. "Come in. You must be frozen."

"I beg your pardon?"

"My middle name is Rainbow. Didn't Fiona tell you?"

"No." He entered, rubbing his hands together, and headed straight for the warmth of the hearth. "It fits you, though. Boy, it's cold. I'm glad you started a fire."

"Me, too, as long as it doesn't wake up more hibernating snakes. Have you had any more sick cattle?"

"No, none."

"Good. I don't know if I could handle another catastrophe right now. I'm really beat."

"How about doing something that will make you feel better?" Michael asked. "I'm about to head to the evening church service Sam mentioned. Would you like to join me? We can grab a bite to eat at Fiona's afterward."

"Thanks but no thanks. I'm still getting over the fancy dinner at the Broadmoor. You go ahead."

Michael shook his head. "Nope. I told you I wasn't going to let you out of my sight for very long. We both go or nobody does." As he spoke, he paused to pet her affectionate blue heeler.

"Be sensible," Layla argued. "There are plenty of people on the ranch who can look out for me, not to mention Smokey there. You don't have to be my shadow. Besides, the bad guy is dead. You said so yourself."

"I'm not about to take the chance he had friends."

"I don't even want to think about it."

"Well, one of us better."

"I suppose you're right." She folded her arms and hugged herself. "Have you heard anything more from Sam? Did you tell him about the snake?"

"Yes."

"What did he say?"

"Only that he thinks we should continue to take precautions."

"That's a no-brainer." She rolled her eyes. "So, what you're telling me is that if I won't go to church with you, you won't go, either?"

"Right."

"Of all the ploys I've ever heard to drag unsuspecting people into church, that's definitely the winner."

"It's not a ploy. It's the truth."

Shaking her head, Layla sighed and began to pace. "You don't understand. Going with you to church will be just like it was at the Broadmoor. I won't belong. I never have."

"I thought you were a Christian."

"I am. What does that have to do with it?"

"Plenty," Michael said. "The congregation at Good Shepherd is special. They'll love you. You'll see."

"Hold it." Layla's eyebrows arched. "You drive all the way into Colorado Springs to go to Good Shepherd? What's wrong with finding a nice church in Cripple Creek?" She saw his countenance darken, his eyes reflect inner sadness.

"My family likes Good Shepherd."

Layla quietly waited for him to explain further. When he didn't, she asked, "What else?"

"I used to go to a little church down the road," he said pensively. "I met someone there."

"Tammy?"

Michael's eyebrows arched. "I see you're up on local gossip."

"Sorry. I didn't pry, honest. It just came up in conversation. I think Holly mentioned it."

"That figures." He sighed deeply, audibly. "The folks at that church are wonderful, too. The place just holds too many memories for me. I prefer to go to Good Shepherd and visit with old friends and family."

"Perfectly logical. Which brings me right back to my original point. There is no part of Colorado Springs society that will ever accept me, period. I've had years of experience trying to fit in without giving up my sense of self. It's never worked."

"Oh yeah?" Michael began to smile.

"Why are you so smug all of a sudden?"

"Me? Smug? Let's just say I'm confident. Tell you what. I'll stand right outside while you get ready so you'll know I haven't phoned ahead and set things up. Come to church with me, if you dare, and I'll prove what an accepting place Good Shepherd is."

"You don't give up, do you?"

"Not in this case. I think you need that chip knocked off your shoulder. For your own good, of course."

"For my own good? Right." She frowned. "Okay, I'll go. But I won't like it."

Michael chuckled. "We'll see. Wear that skirt you had on when we first met. And plenty of your noisy jewelry. Might as well do this up right."

"You are determined to get me ostracized, aren't you? All right. As long as you promise to stay with me and defend me while we're there."

The look on his face was more than self-satisfied, she noted. He was beginning to look positively gleeful.

He raised his right hand, palm out, as if taking a solemn oath. "I promise, Doc. I'll be right by your side the whole time, stuck to you like a burr in a horse's mane, whether you like it or not."

"Now that is a picture I could have done without," Layla replied. "Okay. Wait outside. I'll hurry. I wouldn't want you to freeze to death just to drag me to church."

As Michael left she thought she heard him mutter, "I can't think of a better reason."

"So, Redding's dead. Congratulations. Maybe you'd like to explain to me how that helps our plan."

"It was necessary," *El Jefe* replied.

"I don't see why."

"You'd have seen plenty if he'd talked."

"Led the cops to Ritchie, you mean?"

El Jefe's anger was evident. "It was a whole lot more than that. If Redding knew the mayor's office was in our pocket because of Owen Frost, there's no telling who he might have blabbed to. The fewer stupid street punks we have in on our plans, the better."

His companion nodded. "I see your point."

"Good. Remember who's running this operation."

"You are, Chief. You know I'll always support you in anything you decide to do."

"Then next time, make sure Ritchie knows he'd better take care of matters personally. Or else. We've already had far too many slipups."

"You made Redding's death look like an accident?"

"No. Suicide. The poor guy was despondent over shooting the mayor and nearly killing Vance's vet. He knew he'd be prosecuted and couldn't face the idea of life in prison."

"Will the cops buy that?"

El Jefe cackled. "Of course they will. They don't have a clue who they're up against. They're all idiots."

Looking away to keep from revealing too much critical emotion, the other person kept silent. Idiots? Maybe. Versus the madman Baltasar Escalante had become? Definitely. If they actually got away with all this, alive and wealthy, it wouldn't be because of his masterful plan. It would be in spite of it.

Layla shivered when the headlights of Michael's truck illuminated the broken rail where she'd skidded off SR 67. "Whew. Looks like that was a closer call than I thought. How far down does that canyon go, anyway?"

"You don't want to know."

"I figured as much." She pressed her lips together.

"Someday, we'll have to drive past here in the daylight so I can get a better look."

"It'll make you thankful. I know it did me." He swallowed hard. His hands gripped the wheel tighter. "There are few places along that particular stretch that have enough vegetation to catch you the way those trees did. Your guardian angel probably has gray hair by now."

Layla laughed nervously. "I imagine she's been gray for quite a while, poor thing."

"Meaning you're a risk taker?" Michael kept his eyes on the road except for one split-second glance at her.

"I used to be. I like to think I've matured enough to use caution when it's called for. I wasn't speeding when I ran off the road, you know. That other truck came out of nowhere."

"It sure did." Michael nodded in the direction of a gravel offshoot. "I suspect it was waiting for you on one of the side roads along here. Once the driver spotted your truck, all he had to do was pull out, fall in behind you, and wait till you were in the worst possible position. He had to have been familiar with this road or he wouldn't have been able to identify the most dangerous sections at night."

Answering, Layla was surprised to hear a quaver in her voice. "It still seems unreal, like a bad dream. If I didn't have my truck as proof, I might be able to convince myself it didn't really happen."

"You'd be a lot better off accepting the wreck as a serious warning."

"Do you really think it was?"

Michael's voice deepened. His jaw muscles clenched, accentuating his strong, square chin. "Only a fool would doubt it. There's something weird going on around here and it looks like you and I are involved up to our eyebrows, like it or not."

"I *don't* like it," Layla said flatly. She tried to lighten the somber mood. "Think I could get a good deal if I traded in my old truck for a tank?" To her relief, Michael went along with the silly conversation.

"Colorado Springs does have a military base but I don't think they sell antiquated tanks," he said. "Sam's brother, Travis, is married to Tricia, a retired air force major. We could ask her to find out for us."

"Another useful cousin?" Layla rolled her eyes. "Is there anything your relatives *aren't* involved in?"

"Nope," Michael said, starting to smile. "And my brother is an air force pilot. Now that I give it some thought, we're pretty much into everything, especially regarding Colorado Springs."

"No wonder somebody's out to get you. Who'd you make mad enough to go to all this trouble to hurt you?"

"I beg your pardon?"

"I said, who did you make mad?" She watched a hint of cautious understanding start to shadow Michael's countenance. Clearly, he was engaging in deep introspection.

Finally, he said, "I'm glad you brought that up. There's only one source of evil I can think of that might affect all of us, beginning with Uncle Max."

"What?" Layla swiveled as best she could without removing her seat belt and stared at him. "Who?"

With a determined shake of his head, Michael said, "It happened before you came back to the area. Forget I mentioned it."

Chapter Nine

Layla grew so introspective after her disturbing conversation with Michael, she barely noticed their approach to Good Shepherd Church. She couldn't, however, fail to be impressed by the sight of the old brick edifice, complete with bell tower and graceful spire.

"It's beautiful," she told Michael as he parked in the lot. "That's what churches are supposed to look like."

He smiled. "My, my, Doc. You surprise me. I never took you to be such a traditionalist."

"I can be, in certain instances. Guess it all goes back to growing up around here. I've seen this building lots of times. My mother always admired the stained glass windows."

"From the outside?"

Layla gave him a derisive look. "Yes, from the outside. My folks weren't much for church while we lived in Manitou Springs. I'm thankful they started practicing what they preached after we moved away, though."

Michael held up his hands in mock surrender. "Hey, I wasn't putting anybody down. I just meant the windows are even more dramatic if you see them from the inside, particularly on a sunny day when the light streams in through them."

"Oh." Layla made a face. "Sorry."

"No problem."

Michael got out and circled the truck. By the time he reached the passenger side, Layla had already climbed down and was waiting for him.

He offered his arm. "Watch your step. As cold as it is tonight, there may be fresh patches of ice."

"I'll be careful."

Determined to walk to the door unassisted, she spread her arms like a circus tightrope walker and led the way. Michael was right. The surface of the parking lot did have slick places.

He was hovering as if he expected to have to catch her.

"I'm okay," Layla insisted, pausing only long enough to add, "You don't have to stay so close. Honest."

The words were barely out of her mouth when she placed her right foot on an uneven patch of snow, heard it crackle like cellophane and felt it give beneath her weight. That wasn't worrisome. She'd walked on snowy ground before. She knew what she was doing.

This particular patch of snow hid a sheet of ice suspended above a frigid puddle. When Layla's foot broke through with a splash and hit bottom, it gave her an unexpected jolt.

Overcorrecting to keep her balance, she took a stutter step forward with her opposite foot, which threw her whole body too far forward. The result would have been an awkward fall, had Michael not reached out and grasped her closest, flailing arm.

"Gotcha," he said, hauling her upright. "*Now* will you let me steady you? I'd hate to bring a guest to church and have her break a leg before she even got through the door."

"Whew!" Layla spread her stance slightly for better balance, then gave him a lopsided smile. "Okay. This time. Just don't get any ideas. I'm perfectly capable of taking care of myself. I've been doing it for years."

"I'm sure you have."

Michael held out his hand and Layla took it. He'd left his hat and gloves in the truck but his fingers were still toasty warm, his grip comforting. No one but him had offered her unconditional assistance in a long time. The more she thought about her growing feelings of belonging, the more she realized how lonely she really was.

Sighing, Layla tried to put away the thoughts that were touching her heart so deeply, so unexpectedly. Going to church had never made her want to weep before and she certainly wasn't going to let herself get all teary eyed now. Especially not in front of Michael Vance or his friends and family.

A group of warmly dressed parishioners was entering the wide double doors as Layla and Michael approached. He reached to catch the door before it swung closed. His feet slipped. He lunged, made a grab for the edge of the door.

The next thing Layla knew, he was hanging from the door on one side, from her hand on the other, and she was the one holding *him* up.

"Nice move, cowboy. I thought you were going to keep *me* from falling down?"

"Looks like it was mutual. Thanks. I can't afford broken bones, either."

"You're welcome." The silly, embarrassed look on his face lifted her spirits. "If we weren't already this close, I'd suggest we crawl."

"Very funny." Michael straightened his coat and politely held the door for her. "After you."

Pastor Gabriel Dawson spotted Michael and extended his hand. "Good to see you. Glad you could make it tonight."

Michael shook hands, then made introductions. "This is Layla Dixon, my new vet. Layla, Gabriel Dawson. And over there is his wife, Susan, holding the baby. The cute little twins are Hannah and Sarah. Don't ask me which is which."

Gabriel chuckled pleasantly as he greeted Layla and surveyed his family. "Pleased to meet you, Doctor. As you can see, I am truly blessed. I thought Susan and the girls had completed my family till our Elijah came along. Life just keeps getting better and better."

"The twins are beautiful," Layla said. Their warm, chocolate-colored complexions made them almost glow, and the pretty girls looked adorable in their velvet dresses. The African-American family stood closest to the door, welcoming everyone to Good Shepherd. Hopefully, she had hidden her initial surprise at meeting the tall, handsome pastor.

Michael shepherded Layla into the sanctuary, leaving Gabriel to continue to greet the steady stream of arrivals.

She was amazed at the warmth and acceptance, even affection, she sensed all around her. This *was* a special place, just as Michael had claimed.

Holly spied them from a distance and hurried over. "I don't believe it!" She grasped Layla's hand. "Welcome! Wait till Mom hears."

"I'm glad to see you again, too," Layla said. "Speaking of Marilyn, where is she?"

Holly sobered. "Not here yet. She stopped at the hospital to see Uncle Max and visit with Aunt Lidia."

"Has there been any change?" Michael asked.

"No," Holly said sadly. "It's awful. Poor Aunt Lidia. She just sits there by Max all day and half the night, praying he'll wake up and be okay."

"I don't know either of them but I am sorry about their troubles," Layla said. "I heard the mayor was shot some time ago. Do the police have any leads?"

"Beats me." Holly shrugged and made a grim face. "Brendan won't talk. Neither will Sam. And forget worming anything out of my Jake. Even if he was in a position to hear something, he's too wrapped up in technical jargon to pay attention. My only hope is getting Becca Hilliard to blab. Because she works with Sam, chances are slim and none." Holly brightened. "Which reminds me. Becca was supposed to help in the nursery tonight. She had to work so she called me to sub for her." Cupping her hand to speak aside to Layla, she added, "Becca always says she doesn't want any kids of her own, probably because she already raised her siblings."

Layla giggled. "I'd like children a lot better if they had four legs and fur and wagged their tails."

"You two." Holly rolled her eyes at her brother. "You're so alike it's scary."

Watching the young woman flounce away, Layla shook her head. "Boy, is she wrong."

"Oh? You think so?"

"I know so. Look at us," Layla said. "You're as conventional as can be. You have a great family, lots of friends, a church you call home in spite of the distance you have to drive to get here, a ranch that's been in your family for generations and a plan for the future. I, on the other hand, have none of those things."

"Sure you do. Or you could have."

"Oh?" Layla waggled her eyebrows and shot him a look of disbelief. "My family is spread all over the country and sees no reason to gather for any reason. I haven't been to church since I was a teen. I didn't fit in the cliques then and I still don't. I have no home except my truck, which is now wrecked. And my only plans for the future are to get it repaired so

I can hit the road again. What in the world do you and I have in common?"

"A love of animals and nature, for starters," he said. "And we're both intelligent. We live by a strong moral code, even when it's not easy, because of our mutual beliefs."

"That's hardly enough reason to decide we're alike," Layla argued.

Michael gazed deeply into her eyes as if he was willing her to hear more than his words.

She wanted to look away, to distance herself both physically and emotionally, yet she couldn't force herself to do it. The way Michael was staring at her made her feel as if she were the most loved, most desirable woman in the world.

He gently grasped her fingers and drew her aside. "Listen, Doc. I don't understand what's happening between us any more than I can tell you what's going on with Max and the others. One thing I do know. I aim to do everything in my power to look after you."

Touched, Layla turned to sarcasm rather than allow herself to take his vow seriously. "Oh? Then how about leveling with me? What *else* did Sam say when he shooed me out of the kitchen so you two could talk?"

"It's complicated," Michael said. "Let's go find a seat for the service and try to enjoy ourselves."

"You'll tell me later?" She didn't like his guarded expression so she rephrased with added emphasis. "Let me put it this way, Mr. Vance. You *will* tell me later."

"You are one stubborn lady, you know that?"

"Yup. Looks like that's one more thing you and I have in common. We're both as hardheaded as one of those old muley cows of yours."

"Worse," Michael countered. "The cows don't hardly have the sense to come in out of the rain. You and I are supposed to be a lot smarter than that."

"Meaning we aren't?"

He was shaking his head slowly, thoughtfully. "Maybe I'm not. If I tell you what I suspect is going on, it may be the dumbest move I've ever made."

"Why? Because you're afraid I'll run away from trouble?"

"No," Michael said flatly. "Because I'm afraid you won't."

It surprised Layla to see Pastor Dawson still clad in his black turtleneck, slacks and tweed sport jacket instead of a black robe as he strode to the front of the sanctuary to lead the opening prayer.

Although she bowed her head with the others, she kept one eye open enough to peer through her lashes at Michael. He was surreptitiously eyeing her the same way!

She tried harder to concentrate on the pastor's words while an unspoken prayer of her own shot heavenward. Thankfully, "Amen" followed quickly and she was free to raise an eyebrow at her companion.

"What?" Michael whispered.

Layla shook her head and stifled a smile as they

settled into the pew, side by side. "This church is a lot more casual than I'd anticipated."

"That's because it's the evening service," Michael explained. "On Sunday mornings we're probably every bit as stuffy as you figured we'd be."

"I'd call that formal, not stuffy. In a fancy building like this, I just assumed the service would be…I don't know—more ceremonial?"

"We come here to learn and to praise the Lord." Michael reached for her hand and laced his fingers with hers. "To me, that means any genuine effort is acceptable, with or without formalities."

"You were right about these people being friendly." Layla kept her voice down even though all that was coming from the pulpit at that moment were announcements of upcoming events. "I've lost count of all the ones who've smiled at me and told me they were glad I was here."

"You can add me to that list."

"Thanks. I'm glad I came, too."

"Feels like home, doesn't it?" Michael asked.

Layla's head snapped around. "What makes you say that?"

"Because that's exactly how I feel."

"Doesn't mean *I* do," Layla countered.

Despite her quick denial, however, she did feel at peace here. It was an odd sensation, one she couldn't recall ever having had in a church before today. Of course, she'd never sat in a pew with Michael Vance holding her hand, either. The times she'd attended services with her parents she'd naturally stayed close to them. Later, when her father had decided he didn't care for the church her mother had chosen, they'd simply quit worshipping anywhere.

At that time, Layla had missed church so much she'd trotted off to a nearby Sunday School alone, only to discover that the teens in her age group enjoyed an even more tightly knit social order than their pious parents did.

All in all, Layla had felt totally rejected by everyone except God. It was His love that had saved her, in more ways than one, and it was His love that continued to sustain her.

She squeezed Michael's fingers. "All right. I admit it. This place is special."

His expression softened, grew empathetic. He smiled so tenderly Layla wondered if the mere sight of his unabashed joy was going to make her cry.

Fighting to subdue her emotions, she tilted up her chin, stiffened her spine and forced herself to concentrate on Reverend Dawson's words. That would have been a lot easier if her fingers had not remained entwined with Michael's.

"We are blessed," Gabriel Dawson said. "Let's not forget that with that blessing comes responsibility. Tonight I want to refer to Hebrews twelve, verses fourteen and fifteen. 'Pursue peace with all people, and holiness, without which no one will see the Lord; looking carefully lest anyone fall short of the grace of God, lest any root of bitterness springing up cause trouble; and by this many be defiled.'"

Reverend Dawson paused to gaze fondly over his congregation. "I know it sounds like I'm preaching to the choir, as they say, but sometimes we need to be reminded of how strongly *our* actions can affect another person's walk with God."

Layla felt as if he were speaking directly to her.

"Are you busy?" the pastor went on. "Harried? Too engrossed in daily life to be bothered with other people's problems? It's easy to fall into the trap of thinking that way, to put off doing what your heart tells you to. After all, our time is valuable, isn't it?"

He again scanned the assembled worshippers. "Well, you're right. Your time is precious. Every breath is God given. That's why we owe it to Him to put our lives to good use." His grin widened and lit up his face. "Who's going to be the biggest loser if we're so busy tending to our own business that we can't spare a few minutes to help others? How hard is it to smile, to offer assistance, to encourage a brother or sister who may be feeling down?"

Layla felt Michael's grip tighten momentarily and she glanced at him through lowered lashes. Was that what he was doing? Was he being nice to her because he knew he was expected to? Or did he actually like her for herself? She supposed it could be both. He was probably a kind person with or without his profession of faith.

Yet she did sense something more between them. It was as if an invisible bond had existed from the moment she and Michael had met. All along, she'd been assuming that sense of affinity was due to their mutual love of animals. Now, she had to admit there might be a deeper connection. Was Michael feeling it, too, she wondered, or was her overactive imagination influencing her unduly?

Reverend Dawson continued, "The sad part is, we can go out these doors and into the community, truly intent on making a difference for good, and still miss the point. Love starts at home." He spread his arms wide. "And right here."

Again, he smiled and looked around the sanctuary, reminding Layla of a benevolent father appreciating his many diverse children.

"I think what the writer to the Hebrews was saying is that every pat on the back we fail to give is a missed opportunity to demonstrate God's love, through us. Every person for whom we have no time, is another soul who may go astray simply because we were too busy to show we cared."

Layla's mind wandered as he concluded his short sermon. Could her sense of being an outsider be rooted in her own resentment? Was that what was keeping her from truly belonging anywhere? Instead of her lifestyle and clothing being an expression of her inner self, was she using those differences to stay set apart, to make sure she never let anyone get close enough to hurt her again?

The congregation stood for a closing hymn. Beside her, Michael sang from his heart. The timbre of his voice filled her senses and tickled the fine hairs at her nape while the hall swelled with praise.

A frisson of anticipation and awe skittered

through her. Was this what she'd been missing? Had her innermost heart been trying to tell her all along?

It's just a feeling, Layla argued. *I've always been too easily influenced by my emotions. I can't rely on that.*

No, she reasoned, she couldn't. But she could speak to Reverend Dawson and ask him a few questions about it later. A simple hymn of praise had never before left goose bumps on her arms or filled her heart with such joy. These people *were* set apart, for whatever reason, and she wanted to know how to join in their celebration of life.

Gabriel Dawson called for a closing prayer. It included pleas for those who were sick or had other problems, as well as thanks for previous solutions.

Layla was confused. This group of Christians had just sung as if their hearts and souls were in perfect heavenly agreement, yet now they were listing problem after problem and loss after loss, including Max Vance's continuing coma. How could they be happy in spite of all these shared woes?

The answer came to her in a memorized verse so vivid it might have been spoken from the pulpit. "Trust in the Lord with all your heart and lean not unto your own understanding."

Layla frowned. That was what she'd been doing, wasn't it? She peeked over at Michael. This time, his head was bowed, his eyes fully closed.

Her heart swelled. Her pulse sped. Every sense

was heightened. Every instinct insisted she *must* embrace him.

She resisted, of course. The last thing the poor man needed was to add embarrassment to his already substantial burdens. Besides, she was probably feeling especially loving only because of the pastor's sermon.

The final "Amen" came and Michael looked up at her without speaking. Layla could tell he'd been moved by the closing prayer and she remained quiet to give him time to compose himself.

Others did not seem as aware of his mood. They gathered around to meet Layla before leaving the church, jabbering and offering hugs and handshakes as if she were a long-lost sister.

She responded as best she could while Michael made introductions. Finally, he placed his hand at the small of her back and guided her toward a side door instead of the center aisle.

"Let's go this way," he said. "It's less crowded."

"Suits me. Whew! When they hear a sermon about being friendly, they sure take it to heart."

"Told you so. It doesn't take one of Gabriel's pep talks to motivate most of them, though."

"I noticed that the minute we walked in the door." Layla smiled at him. "Did you forget, or do you just want to hear me say it again?"

"Say what?"

She could tell from the mischievous twinkle in his dark eyes that he was teasing. "That you were right."

"It is music to my ears," Michael quipped. They

rounded a corner together and he stopped abruptly. "There's Sam. Wait here, will you? I need to clear something with him. I'll be right back."

"You mean the deep, dark secrets you promised to tell me?"

"Yes. I don't want to do or say anything that might jeopardize any police investigations. Getting the bad guys and locking them up where they can't do any more damage is the most important thing."

Layla placed her hand on his arm to momentarily delay him. "I'd much rather know up front who my enemies are."

Sighing and nodding, Michael patted her hand. "Yeah. Me, too. That's why I still intend to teach you how to properly handle a gun."

"I told you, I don't need that kind of protection."

"You also told me you weren't worried about driving home alone on an icy mountain road, and look what that got you. Not to mention the snake in the bathroom."

Layla made a face. "Don't remind me."

"Somebody better," Michael countered. "What good is it to know who your enemies are if you can't defend yourself against them?"

"I thought we were supposed to trust the Lord for our protection."

"I trust Him to have provided the means for me to take care of myself and my family," he said. "If I sit back and don't lift a finger, it's like the foolish servant who buried the coins he was given in the ground rather than put them to work. It's my responsibility to use what I have to take care of those I care about."

His words dived deep into Layla's heart and echoed there. Was he saying he had romantic feelings for her or was he simply using that term to express concern? It could be either.

She opened her mouth, intending to ask Michael to clarify, then changed her mind. She didn't want to know how he felt about her because it might force her to reconsider her own feelings for him. They were considerable…and confusing. Admiration likely topped the list but that sentiment was all mixed up with tenderness and friendship and camaraderie and who knows what else.

Could she be falling in love with him? Layla wondered. Maybe. No, probably. She swallowed past the dry, cottony lump in her throat with great effort. There should have been doubts, excuses, yet none surfaced.

Michael's hand still lay atop hers where she'd grasped his arm. His touch was warm, his calloused hand proof of his hardworking lifestyle. She raised her eyes to meet his and imagined she saw a reflection of the feelings he'd mentioned. Just as she was about to deny its existence, Michael closed his fingers around hers and gave them a gentle squeeze.

"Wait here," he said softly. "I'll be right back."

Watching him hail Sam and hurry toward him, Layla was struck by the reality of her emotional attachment. She didn't want to be away from Michael.

Not for one second. The urge to run to catch up to him was so strong she was nearly overcome by it.

Shuffling her feet, she forced herself to wait and watch. She couldn't hear what was being said but Michael was gesturing and Sam was shaking his head. That was not a good sign. Neither was the slump of Michael's broad shoulders.

As he turned and started back to her, Layla could tell she wasn't going to learn much more than she already knew.

"He told you to keep me in the dark, didn't he?" she asked as soon as Michael rejoined her.

"Not exactly. He did warn me not to jump to the wrong conclusions, though."

"Which were?"

Michael gave her a lopsided smile. "Even if I told you, you'd still be as mystified as I am."

"That wouldn't be hard. I'm already pretty confused." She made a silly face. "I don't have the kind of mind that can take clues and puzzle them out. I love to read mystery stories or watch movies like that, but I'm always the last one to figure them out."

"You have a creative mind. I'm analytical. Those aren't faults, they're differences in the way we think."

Layla smiled. "Thanks. I needed that."

"You're welcome. Am I forgiven?"

"For what? You leveled with me. You told me the truth. I can hardly ask for more."

"But you'd like to?"

Her grin widened, her eyes sparkled. "You said

you knew me pretty well already. What do you think?"

Michael laughed. "I think it's time we made tracks for Fiona's. You need to be distracted."

Though Layla joined in his laughter as she accompanied him to his truck, she knew nothing could distract her from the confusion that had settled in her heart. She wasn't fretting about the danger they might face or remembering the narrow escapes they'd already had. Her bewilderment went far deeper. It was based in the feelings she'd kept denying. And those feelings were tangled up with the vision she kept having of becoming a permanent part of Michael Vance's life.

That was nothing but wishful thinking, of course. No matter how close their trials had brought them, the outside stimulus was temporary. The best she could hope for was a good letter of reference and perhaps a lingering friendship, a place to stop and visit the next time she passed through this part of Colorado.

Always before, that tenuous connection to others had been more than enough to satisfy Layla. Now, the idea of saying goodbye to Michael and his enormous extended family made her heart ache. What was wrong with her?

She gritted her teeth. Okay, so she had stupidly allowed herself to fall in love with the wrong man. That mistake she could accept without question. But what about the remainder of her emotional conflict? It involved other people who were part of Michael's life, people whose presence had blessed her and continued to do so. How had *that* happened?

More importantly, how was she going to keep them at arm's length, where they belonged, when they were already so entrenched in her heart of hearts that she was beginning to think of them as her own family?

Chapter Ten

By the time Michael took Layla to Fiona's, as he'd promised, it was after 8:00 p.m.

Layla seemed amazed that the Stagecoach Café was so busy. "You should be glad you live in a place where you can eat out this late," she remarked. "Some of the little towns I've visited roll up their sidewalks early, especially on Sunday."

"I guess there are advantages to a big city. I wouldn't want to actually live here, though."

"Neither would I."

Her statement saddened him. No matter how often he heard her affirm her wanderlust, it still gave him a jolt.

"So, where do you plan to go after you leave Cripple Creek?" he asked.

Layla shrugged. "I don't know. Maybe I'll head back down south. The Ozarks are pretty in the spring."

"So are the Rockies," Michael said. "We'll have wildflowers poking through the snow soon."

"Do you have dogwood trees?"

"I don't think so. Sorry."

"They grow wild in the Ozarks, with big, white flowers that bloom before the forest leafs out, so that's all you see. They're really beautiful."

He had to stop himself from offering to plant a grove of dogwoods just for her. He'd already said plenty when he'd carelessly let slip how much he cared about her. There was no use making things worse. Honesty might be the best policy but it could also be plenty embarrassing. Especially if a guy was stupid enough to mention his feelings to a woman who kept making it clear she didn't intend to stick around any longer than necessary.

Michael led the way to an unoccupied booth in the rear of the café and slid into the seat opposite Layla before he said, "I suppose I'd better call around tomorrow and see about getting your truck repaired."

"I suppose so." She spread her napkin across her lap and folded her hands. "I hope it's not beyond fixing. That old truck and I've had some great times together."

"And Smokey?"

"Yes, Smokey, too. Although he and I haven't been traveling companions for very long." She smiled wistfully. "I found him at a rest stop in Texas. After I fed him and doctored his sore feet, I stayed in the area for a few weeks, helping out at a local veterinary clinic, while I advertised for his owner. By that time, he and I had really bonded."

"Was that when he ate the sleeves from your jacket?"

Layla laughed. "Yes. Lucky for us, nobody answered my ads and I got to keep him."

"Is that how you support yourself? Working wherever you land?"

"Mostly. My needs are simple. I like having the chance to see the sights and help people and animals at the same time." She smiled across at him. "Like here. If I hadn't been passing through, I wouldn't have had the opportunity to help you track down what was killing your cattle."

"That's true." Had her hands been resting on the table, Michael would have reached for one of them. "I hope I've thanked you sufficiently."

"You have. And I hope my cooking hasn't been too big a disappointment. I told you I was a granola and yogurt eater when we met."

"That you did." He hailed a passing waitress. "Is Fiona in tonight?"

"No, sir," the young woman said. "She went home after lunch. I'll be back to take your orders in a jiffy."

"No hurry," Michael said. "We're not in any rush."

Settling back against the booth he studied his companion. Layla looked as lovely as ever, yet there was unspoken concern in her expression. "You okay?"

"I was just thinking."

"Uh-oh." He was pleased to see his teasing bring a smile.

"Cut it out, cowboy. I'm serious."

"About what?"

"Something your pastor said. I've been a Christian since I was twelve years old, but he made me feel as if I'm still missing something."

"Like what?"

Layla snickered wryly. "Hey, if I knew that, I wouldn't have to try so hard to figure things out."

"Maybe you should talk to Gabriel. He's a perceptive guy. He's helped me a lot."

"You?" She scowled. "About what? You've already got it together."

"Now, maybe. After Tammy jilted me I was a mess. It was Fiona who finally shamed me into going for counseling. I was sure I could handle things myself. Bless her heart, Fiona saw that I couldn't."

"I suppose your mother and sister kept insisting everything had happened for the best."

"Exactly. Nobody understood how miserable I was. Not even Ken."

"Who's Ken? Another cousin?"

Michael shook his head. "No. Ken's my baby brother. Holly's twin."

"You're kidding! Why hasn't anybody mentioned him?"

"I don't know. He's the one in the air force, so he doesn't really get that involved in the rest of our lives."

"That's too bad. My brother is kind of the same way."

A lot of things are too bad, Michael mused.

Letting Layla go promised to be the hardest thing

he'd had to do in a long, long time. He only hoped he'd be able to bid her farewell without making her feel guilty about leaving. She was a free spirit. He wasn't going to try to cage her. That would destroy everything about her that was so special.

Yeah, he told himself cynically. It was better to bear the burden himself than to let on how desperately he wanted her to stay at the Double V. It was the right thing to do, for her sake, but it was getting harder and harder to accept as inevitable.

If Layla could have said she was merely confused in the days that followed, she'd have been more than satisfied. As it was, she was so perplexed she viewed normal daily puzzlement as a state of mind to be envied.

Part of the problem was her lack of options. There was no way she could get back to Colorado Springs on her own to talk to Reverend Dawson unless she asked Michael to take her, and that was out, period. Whatever was bothering her was at least partly Michael's fault. It had to be. She just wasn't ready to admit it, especially not to him.

Before she'd met the enigmatic rancher she was happy. Content. Satisfied with her life and sure her faith was complete. Now, all that had changed. Thoughts of returning to her wandering ways no longer kindled enthusiasm and a sense of adventure the way they once had. Like it or not, she didn't want to leave the Double V—or its owner.

Disgusted with herself, Layla finished washing up

after breakfast, dressed warmly and made her way to the barn where the horses were stabled.

Norberto was working there and nodded politely as she entered. *"Buenos dias, señorita."*

"Good morning," Layla said with a smile. "I'm glad you're here. Which horse do you recommend I ride?"

He shrugged. "What did Señor Vance say?"

"He just told me I could ride any time I wanted. He didn't warn about any troublesome horses." She approached the stall where the gray, Arab-cross mare was housed. "How about this one? Is she pretty gentle?"

"Si."

The wiry, older man's hesitation bothered her enough to prompt more questions. "Then what's the matter? She looks sound. Is there some reason I shouldn't take her out?"

The ranch manager hesitated. "I don't know, *señorita*—"

"You do, too, know," Layla countered, "so stop pretending. I don't buy that laid-back, unconcerned attitude from your boss and I'm not about to believe it from you, either. What's wrong with this horse?"

Sobering, Norberto leaned on the handle of his pitchfork and answered slowly. "Señor Vance bought her for his other lady. The one who ran away. Nobody else has ridden her, not since..."

"Since Tammy split?" Layla made a face. "What a waste of a good mount. The poor mare is probably so barn-sour she won't do anything for me."

"We have other horses. Nice ones. Let me show you."

Layla had already begun stroking the mare's velvety nose, mumbling to her. She paused long enough to turn to Norberto. "Bring me a saddle and bridle. I'll brush her and clean her feet so she's used to me, then I'll take her out and work her. It'll be good for both of us."

"Yes, ma'am." The ranch manager's leathery face crinkled in a smile so broad it lifted the ends of his mustache. "It will be good for Señor Vance, too, I think."

Layla returned the grin and gave him a reassuring nod. "I agree, Norberto. This horse isn't the only critter on the Double V who needs a little attitude adjustment."

"She went *where?*" Michael was shouting.

"Riding, boss. She said you gave her permission."

"I did. I just never dreamed she'd take a horse out alone. Not when we're still trying to figure out who's been causing all the trouble around here." He grabbed a bridle off a nearby peg and headed for the Appaloosa's stall. "Get my saddle. And the walkie-talkies. I want you listening, in case we need to call for more help."

Norberto did as he was told. "She rides well, boss. Like she is part of the mare. I would not worry."

"Well, *I* do. Which way did she go?" Michael had slipped the bit in the big gelding's mouth and was buckling the leather strap at its cheek.

"South, I think. You should be able to follow her tracks. There is a lot of snow left."

Michael's jaw clenched. His eyes narrowed. The Appaloosa was beginning to shift and prance as it sensed his nervousness. He took a deep, settling breath and worked on getting his temper under control.

"I'll find her," Michael vowed. He gave the saddle girth one final tug and tucked the loose end of the strap through the ring to secure it before letting down the stirrup.

As he swung into the saddle he saw Norberto making the sign of the cross.

"Good idea," Michael said. "And if my mother calls, tell her I've gone out to check the herd."

"You don't want her to know what's going on?"

"No, not yet. There'll be plenty of time for Mom to worry if this turns sour on me." He reined the gelding toward the open barn door and pushed his hat lower on his forehead to keep it in place. "Listen to your radio. I'll call if I find Layla."

Breaking into the open and starting to canter, Michael added, "*When* I find her."

That thought hit him like a literal punch in the stomach. He *would* find her. He had to. The alternative was unthinkable.

Layla was delighted at the progress she and the mare, whom she'd named "Fatima," were making. A gentle hand on the reins or a touch of her heels was all it now took to elicit a suitable response. The horses on which she'd learned to ride were nothing like this fine mount. She didn't wonder why Michael had chosen Fatima for Tammy. The question was, why had he left such a magnificent horse to languish in the barn? It certainly wasn't the mare's fault that Tammy had turned out to be disloyal. And if the sight of the horse had bothered him that much, why hadn't he sold or traded her?

Leaning forward in the saddle, Layla patted Fatima's elegantly arched neck. Arabians were a breed that always reminded her of a prancing carousel steed, full of grace and fluid beauty with a touch of inherent excitement.

Though Layla was familiar with the overall lay of the land, she took pains to keep an eye on Pike's Peak so she'd be certain of her direction in relation to the Double V. Peace lay across the high country like the blanket of fluffy snow that wrapped the hills, giving Layla the respite she craved. There was something soothing about the steady, rocking cadence of a horse's gait, the creaking leather of the saddle beneath her.

"And the presence of God in all nature," Layla added aloud. Michael understood that feeling as well as she did. It was one of the things she liked about him.

She stretched to loosen some of the knots in her neck and shoulders while she pictured her boss. There was actually a lot to like about Michael Vance, starting with his kind eyes and the gentleness she'd discovered hidden beneath his facade. He played the

part of a crusty, grumpy rancher with total believabil-
ity until you got to know him. Then, it was a different story.

Clouds obscured the sun. Layla was so engrossed
in her assessment of Michael she barely noticed,
other than to shiver when deprived of the sun's
warmth.

Suddenly, Fatima paused, shifted into a sideways,
prancing gait and looked back. Condensation blew
from the mare's nostrils; it's upper lip vibrated with
a soft, nickering call.

"What is it, girl?"

Pivoting to better follow the mare's line of sight,
she saw an unidentifiable horseman approaching at
full gallop.

Layla gave a quick, light tug on the reins. "Whoa.
Easy, girl, easy."

The more she tried to calm the nervously prancing
animal, the more agitated it became. Finally, she
heeded the horse's instinctive urge to escape, dug the
soft heels of her moccasins into its sides and gave it
its head.

Fatima leaped into action and took off, reminding Layla of the flight of a hapless heroine in an old
Western movie. She couldn't help wondering if that
was exactly what was going on. Leaning into the
wind, she matched the horse's cadence till they were
in perfect sync.

Her heart was pounding like the beating hooves
beneath her. Gasps of air whooshing from both Layla
and the mare made visible clouds of condensation in

the icy air. She hunched lower over the saddle horn and hung on with one hand, lest the galloping Arabian make an unexpected course correction and unseat her.

Finally, she chanced a peek over her shoulder. The other rider was rapidly gaining ground!

Michael couldn't believe his eyes. He'd no sooner spotted Layla than she'd taken off like a shot. What could have gotten into her? Was the mare so unused to being ridden that she'd bolted, taking Layla along for the wild ride?

More concerned than ever, he urged the Appaloosa ahead. The little Arab mare might be faster, stride for stride, but his mount had a definite size advantage.

Michael knew the lay of the land, too. What looked like relatively flat terrain was actually a gradual upslope. At this elevation, the stress on their horses would be greatly magnified. Even if he didn't manage to overtake Layla right away, she'd soon be slowing down. It was inevitable.

Hoping she could hear him over the sounds of rushing wind and galloping hooves, he shouted, "Layla, stop! It's me, Michael."

The gray mare dropped into a trot, then a walk. Relieved, Michael continued his rapid advance till the horses were nearly head-to-head. Furious, he leaned to one side, closed his fist around the mare's reins just below her bit and held tight.

"What were you trying to do," he shouted, "kill this horse?"

"Of course not!" She glared at him. "What were *you* trying to do, scare me to death?"

"You're the one who rode out here alone, in spite of my warnings. If you were scared, you deserved it."

"Oh, thanks a heap. I suppose you're going to tell me again that the only place I'll be safe is under your thumb. Why don't you just lock me up and be done with it?"

"Don't tempt me."

Michael knew he shouldn't be yelling at her but he'd been so worried he was barely rational. Layla might not realize how unforgiving the open range could be, but he knew. More than one cow had frozen to death within sight of food and shelter. If his blond companion had been bucked off and had had to walk home, she could have succumbed to hypothermia long before she reached safety. The idea of anything bad happening to this stubborn woman was gut-wrenching.

He'd obviously alienated her. *Well, tough.* She was the one who'd pulled the bonehead stunt and risked her life unnecessarily, not him.

Starting to calm down, he released his hold on the mare's reins, took a deep breath and tried to sound nonchalant. "Where were you headed?"

"I don't know. I thought maybe Fatima and I could find some clues to whoever has been sneaking around, like tire tracks or something."

"Fatima?" He eyed the Arabian. "Never mind. I get it." Tipping his hat back with one finger Michael scanned the darkening sky. "Weather's changing.

Looks like it'll snow soon. We should be starting back."

"Not until we rest these poor horses," Layla countered. She bent to stroke the mare's lathered neck. "I'm sorry I pushed her so hard."

Michael wanted to say, *You should be,* but thought better of it. Instead, he merely nodded and dismounted. "Get down. We'll walk them a ways, then head for home."

When Layla joined him, she seemed a bit shaky. Michael stopped himself from taking her arm to steady her and realized she'd seen him reach out, then draw back.

"I'm okay," Layla said. "I'm just not used to riding. It's been a long time since I've galloped like that. Fatima's a magnificent mare. I'm very impressed."

"Thanks."

"Norberto told me why you bought her. What I don't understand is why no one ever rides her."

"There hasn't been a need," he answered. "While you're here, why don't you consider her yours?"

"Really?"

"Yes." Michael couldn't help grinning at her wide-cyed, childlike enthusiasm. "This may be a first," he quipped. "You're not arguing with me."

"Not this time, cowboy. For once, I think you've come up with an excellent idea."

"Just for once?"

She made a silly face. "Don't push it, okay?"

Laughing and nodding, he said, "Okay."

Chapter Eleven

Snow soon began to fall as Michael had predicted. With the temperature barely at freezing, it formed into wet clumps and smacked like gobs of soft hail instead of drifting gracefully to the ground.

Layla shivered in the saddle as she tried to bat the moisture out of her hair. "Yuck. I almost wish it would rain instead of this sticky stuff."

"I don't suppose you brought a slicker."

"No," she said wryly. "Did you?"

"I left in kind of a hurry. All I had time to grab was the two-way radio I just used to tell Norberto you were safe."

"I'm glad you thought of that. I wouldn't want the poor man to worry."

"You didn't seem to mind worrying *me*."

She gave him a smug, half smile. "I figured you could handle it. I stayed on your property, didn't I?"

"Yes." Michael swung his arm in a wide arc. "All this is Double V land."

"You know every inch of it?"

"Pretty close. Why?"

"I thought I saw a cave on my way out here. Maybe we could take shelter there, at least until the worst of this nasty snow is over." Her smile grew more demure. "That is, if you'll promise to behave."

"Have I ever been anything but a gentleman?" Michael asked, sounding a little perturbed.

"No. You've been wonderful. I just didn't want you to think *I* was making a pass." As much to reassure herself as her companion, she added, "I'm not."

"I know." Stretching in the saddle, he studied the surrounding hills. "What you saw was probably an abandoned mine tunnel. They're thick in these parts. Hundreds are left over from the times when all anybody was interested in was silver mining."

He urged his horse into the lead. "Follow me. It's not far to a mine entrance big enough to give us a place to wait out the bad weather."

Trotting along behind, she couldn't help but watch Michael ride. He was a marvelous horseman. Strong, self-confident, athletic...and devastatingly attractive.

Layla sensed a blush rising to warm her cheeks. Too bad that was the only part of her that didn't feel like it was about to freeze solid. She didn't know when she'd been this cold, this miserable.

Whether she liked hearing it or not, Michael had

been right to chastise her for leaving the barn so un-prepared. She'd lived in Colorado during the winter. She knew how unforgiving the climate could be and how quickly it could change from sunshine to storms. Any fool who'd venture out without proper preparation *deserved* to have icicles in her hair!

Now that she was seeing the mine up close, Layla could tell the entrance was little more than an alcove. Rotting timbers framed the doorway. Less than twenty feet inside lay a pile of coarse rock that looked as if it had dropped from a similar-size cavity in the roof of the shaft.

Michael dismounted and once again grasped the mare's reins. This time, Layla didn't object.

She swung down, said, "Thanks," and sidled past him into the dry recess.

Michael followed, leading both horses. "Don't go too far," he warned. "Last time I looked, there was a pretty sheer drop-off on the other side of that rock slide."

"Why do you leave it open if it's dangerous?" Layla tucked herself behind the horses, out of the wind, and rubbed her icy hands on her sweater-clad upper arms to try to warm them with friction.

"It's only a danger if somebody's out here who doesn't belong," he answered. "All my men are aware of the hazards."

Joining her, he removed his leather coat and wrapped it around her shoulders. His kindness reminded Layla of the way he'd gently looked after her the night she'd been forced off the highway.

"You should keep your jacket," she said. "There's no sense both of us freezing."

"I'm fine for now," Michael said. "I'm not wet like you are. As soon as you get warmer I'll reclaim the coat."

"O-okay."

There was little Layla could do to squelch the shivers skittering along her spine and tickling the back of her neck. If she hadn't been so chilled she'd have assumed she was trembling due to Michael's nearness. As it was, she couldn't be totally certain why she had the shakes. The good part was, neither could the handsome rancher.

"S-sorry," she stammered. "I don't usually get c-cold this easily."

"You don't stand outside in an ice storm often either, I hope."

He gave her a look she interpreted as condescending and she responded with sarcasm. "Sure, I d-do. You know how it is w-with us crazy nature l-lovers. We'll try a-anything we think will bring us closer to the n-natural world."

Instead of laughing the way she'd expected him to, Michael studied her expression. His scrutiny was unnerving.

"What?" Layla asked, giving her damp hair a flip to get it off her forehead. "Haven't you ever seen a hippie-sicle before."

"Not such a beautiful one."

His answer was softly spoken. Its timbre made Layla tingle. This time, there was no question what had sent a frisson of nervousness along her spine.

She blinked to try to clear her head. "Beautiful? Me? Hah! I must look like a drowned rat."

Michael stepped closer. "I wouldn't have put it quite that bluntly."

"Oh?" She tried to back away, found herself bumping into the gray mare's shoulder and stopped. "How would you have put it?"

Raising his hand slowly, Michael cupped her face in his warm palm. His thumb stroked her cheek. "I'd have said you were beautiful all the time, no matter what. You are, you know. And that beauty is a lot more than skin-deep. It goes all the way to your heart."

She wanted to run. Wanted to stay. Wanted to giggle and turn his compliments into another joke instead of taking them seriously. The intensity of his gaze was overpowering. So was the fact she believed he meant every word.

"I—I thought you promised to behave," she said.

"I did. I do. There's nothing wrong with telling you I think you're beautiful when it's the truth."

"Well…"

Layla wondered if the only thing that had kept her from falling into Michael's arms already was the iciness of her stiff muscles. That was a distinct possibility, since it was starting to feel awfully warm in there and her knees were beginning to wobble as if they were about to drop her into a helpless pile of slush at his feet.

Imagining that silly scenario was nearly enough to snap Layla out of the dreamy world Michael Vance's nearness had caused. Nearly, but not quite.

She wished she were the heroine in an old Western movie so she could count on having the gray mare give her a nudge from behind at the right moment.

Imagining that scenario, Layla stepped straight into Michael's arms without further rational thought.

He caught her, enfolded her in his warm, sturdy embrace.

She raised her face to his, her lips slightly parted. She could feel the tension crackling like static electricity between them. There was no doubt he wanted to kiss her. And no matter how she'd protested and warned him beforehand, she wanted it, too.

His breath was warm on her face. His lips were mere inches from hers.

"Fatima pushed me?" she whispered.

"Um-hum."

"Well, she could have. I'm sure she was planning to."

"Was she?"

Layla nodded. She raised on tiptoe and slipped her arms around Michael's neck. "Remember that promise you made?"

"About being a gentleman?"

"Uh-huh. I might overlook one little kiss."

Michael's eyes smiled into hers. "Think so?"

Their lips met, lightly, tenderly. She was so dizzy and overcome with conflicting emotions when he finally leaned away, all she could do was nod and make a muffled sound that reminded her of a happy kitten.

"How was that?" he asked.

"Nice." She sighed. "But short. Really short. I almost missed it. Could we try one more time?"

Michael took off his hat, then swept her into a more possessive embrace and kissed her again.

By the time he released her this time, Layla was breathless. So was he. She blinked and grinned up at him. "Wow. Good job, cowboy."

He backed away, looking contrite and rather unsettled. Layla was positive he was blushing when he said, "My pleasure, ma'am."

Michael had decided halfway through kissing Layla that they'd better not spend any more time alone than they absolutely had to. He'd retrieved the radio from his coat pocket and had asked Norberto to pick them up in one of the ranch trucks ASAP.

While they waited, Michael made small talk to take his mind off thoughts he knew he shouldn't be entertaining. "So, what do you think of my ranch?"

"It's sure big. A person could get lost out here."

"Distances can be deceiving. I'm glad you didn't try to bring Smokey along today."

"Me, too. I might have, if I'd been sure he'd follow me when I was on horseback. I've never tried that before."

"How's he adjusting to the cabin?"

"Pretty well." Layla peered through the falling

snow. "He and King met by accident the other day and neither of them drew blood."

"Good."

"That's what I thought. Poor Molly cowered and hid behind me but nothing bad happened. The males just circled each other and did a lot of posturing, then made their peace."

"I wish people had that much sense," Michael said. "Holding grudges is bad for everybody."

"Especially when they're directed at your friends and family?"

"Yeah. Especially then." He paced to burn excess energy and warm himself up.

Layla took off the coat and held it out to him. "Here. I'm fine now. Really. I feel terrible seeing you shiver like that."

"Then don't look."

Michael knew he sounded unduly annoyed but figured that emotion was safer than some of the others he'd had lately. Kissing Layla had been a big mistake. He'd liked it too much. Worse, he could tell she had, too. Getting romantically involved, given their differences, would do neither of them any good.

Then again, maybe there was hope. She did seem to like living on the Double V. Could she get used to staying in one place if she stuck around longer? He figured it was worth making the effort to find out.

"I meant to tell you," Michael said. "I got a few rough estimates on repairs to your truck."

Layla grimaced. "Do I want to hear how high they were?"

"Probably not."

"That's what I was afraid of."

"I've been thinking," he said. "We've never discussed your wages. Shall we say I pay you by having your truck fixed, plus a little extra per diem?"

"You'd do that?"

"Sure. Why not?"

"Because I'm positive those repairs will cost a lot more than you'd have to lay out if you gave me all cash."

"I don't mind," Michael said, feeling guilty for having offered when his motives weren't totally pure. As long as he had control of that truck of hers, he could delay her departure almost indefinitely.

"Okay, then. It's a deal." She held out her hand.

Instead of shaking hands with her, Michael took his jacket and shrugged into it. "I hear a truck coming. You ride home with Norberto. I'll follow with the horses."

"But—"

"Don't argue, Doc. You may be our official cow mumbler but I'm still the boss around here."

Layla frowned. "Yes, sir. I'll be waiting in the barn to rub Fatima down when you get her home."

"No." Michael shook his head and gave her the sternest look he could muster. "You fix supper. Norberto and I will take care of the horses."

And I won't have to look at you and think about that kiss, he added, furious with himself. Their silly first kiss had started out as innocent fun. Then, before he'd realized things were spiraling out of hand, it had escalated into something more. Much more. Too bad he couldn't take back the entire afternoon and forget how Layla had felt in his arms.

Snorting in disgust, Michael swung into the saddle. He might forget many things in the course of his life but he knew he'd never stop thinking about Layla Dixon. No matter what finally happened, where she went or what shc did, shc'd always have a special place in his heart.

His fondest wish was that she, too, would remember him with affection.

"They can't be that smart," *El Jefe* shouted. "It's impossible."

"Nevertheless, they were seen," his companion answered. "If you don't believe me…"

"I didn't say that. I just can't imagine how they'd know." His fist smacked into his opposite palm, accentuating his pacing gait.

"Maybe they didn't. Maybe they were lucky."

"Luck has nothing to do with this," *El Jefe* insisted. "My intellect is no match for theirs—any of theirs. Even as a team they don't stand a chance against me."

The other person's tone was cajoling. "Of course they don't. I wouldn't worry. We can have the operation out there cleaned up in no time. That way, if they do decide to look into it further, they won't find a thing."

"Don't bother." *El Jefe*'s tone was prideful. "I can see no reason to take extra measures. I've eluded them so far. I'll continue to do so." He dismissed concern with a wave of the hand. "Never underestimate me."

"Of course not. You are *El Jefe*, The Chief. No one comes close to you. Your cunning is legendary."

A cackling laugh echoed in the cavernous room. "I am more than a legend," *El Jefe* said. "I am a spirit. An avenger that can't be touched. Ask anyone in the Vance or Montgomery families. They'll tell you how much Baltasar Escalante was—is—feared."

"And I am your humble servant. Your devoted ally. Should I fear you, too?" his companion asked.

Dark eyes narrowed to slits as *El Jefe* met the other's gaze. "Only if you try to double-cross me. Many have tried. Many have died for their foolishness." His lips curled with self-satisfied scorn. "Many more will go to their graves ruing the day they acted against me."

"Like Ritchie's friend, you mean?"

"That was just a taste of how I reward failure. I will not let anything, or anyone, stop me."

Nodding, his companion forced a complacent, submissive smile. "Whatever I can do to help, just ask. What is mine is yours. I am at your service."

"You'd better be," *El Jefe* warned. "Anyone who isn't loyal will face the consequences by my own hand."

Layla hunkered down in the truck cab beside Norberto and held her fingers in front of the warm air from the heater. "Br-r-r. It's freezing out there."

"*Si, señorita.*"

"I hope you didn't get in trouble for letting me take the mare out."

The wiry older man shrugged. "No *problemo.*"

"Yeah, well, there was plenty of *problemo* when your boss caught up to me. Boy, was he steamed!"

"It is good for him," Norberto replied.

Layla arched a brow and swiveled to look behind the slow-moving truck. Michael had turned up the fleece-lined collar of his heavy coat and pulled his hat low over his forehead to block some of the wind, but he was clearly very cold. She saw him leave the wider track that the truck was following and start across the open range, apparently making a beeline for the barn.

"Why is it good?" She could see emotion in the ranch hand's face, emotion she imagined might be affection. When he spoke, she was sure.

"Because Señor Vance has not cared in a long time. Not since that woman left. It is good for him to feel. To worry. It is a healthy thing."

"You mean instead of bottling it up inside?"

"No." Norberto was shaking his head when he glanced over at her. A smile was lifting the ends of his mustache. "I mean it is good to see him interested in someone again. Someone like you, who will be good for him."

"Whoa! Hold your horses, mister. I'm the last person who'd be good for Michael—I mean, Mr. Vance. I'm glad to hear he's healing from whatever Tammy did, but I'm certainly not in line to take her place."

"Will you be his friend?"

"Of course. I already am."

"Then that is enough. The other woman, she was never his friend. She had different plans. Everybody could see that but Señor Vance. I think she was always after his money, maybe as a way to get what she really wanted."

Layla gave a subdued sigh and faced forward. "I suppose he is rich. I hadn't really thought about it. He'd have to have a lot of money to be able to support a place like this, especially the way cattle prices fluctuate."

"*Si*. And there is the mining, too."

"Mining? The way he talked, I assumed all the silver had played out."

"There are still mineral rights to lease."

"Are they worth a lot?"

"Not as much as water. Any rancher who needs water and doesn't have the rights has a hard time here in Colorado. The state controls who gets water and how much." He bent to take a better look at the cloud-laden sky. "This is good for the land. Not so much runs off if it melts slowly."

"There's apparently a lot I don't know about this part of the country," Layla said.

Norberto gave her a fatherly smile. "You will learn, *señorita*. You are smart. And you are interested. The rest will come naturally."

Thinking about how hard she'd had to work to learn to cook, Layla chuckled. "I don't know about that. I imagine Michael will be really glad when your wife is back on her feet and able to start working in the house again."

To her surprise, the older man abruptly looked away. She scowled. "Norberto? How *is* Imelda doing?"

"She is better, I think."

Layla thought she noted a twitch of a smile at the corner of his mouth but with such a thick mustache covering his lip, it was hard to be certain.

"How much better?"

Norberto shrugged.

His I-don't-know attitude gave Layla pause. Could Imelda be stalling for reasons other than wanting to be pampered? She supposed it was possible. Norberto was certainly hiding something.

The real question was, was Michael aware of the suspicious circumstances surrounding his cook's extended absence? She doubted it. No man who liked to eat meat as much as Michael Vance did would purposely replace Imelda with someone who regarded beef as inedible.

Layla smiled to herself. If he was stringing her along just to keep her at the Double V, then he deserved to go hungry. And if Norberto and Imelda were pulling the wool over everyone else's eyes, whatever their motive, the truth would come out soon enough.

She folded her arms across her chest and set her jaw. Until the facts became evident, she'd keep fixing healthy food and watching Michael struggle to eat it. He'd been doing pretty well, considering. And he was undoubtedly more fit because of the change in his diet, so all her efforts were not in vain.

She pictured him seated across from her at the kitchen table. The image of the two of them, together, seemed so right, so perfect, it made Layla's heart beat faster.

She licked her lips. Thought of Michael's kiss. Remembered the look in his eyes. It was clearly one of love. She couldn't deny that. What she could deny—must deny—was that she shared those tender feelings.

Chapter Twelve

By the time they arrived at the ranch house the snow had stopped. Boot tracks led up to the back door. It looked as though Michael had beaten them home.

Layla was halfway to the house when Norberto caught up to her. "Wait, *señorita*. I will check inside for you."

Her brows arched and she faced him. "What for? Did your boss tell you I have to be watched all the time?"

The older man looked confused. "No, no. It is not you. It is a…" He struggled for the word.

"Precaution?" Layla offered.

"*Si*. A precaution."

"Well, you can stop fussing over me. Michael's home. See his footprints? He's already gone into the house."

Norberto's eyes narrowed. Glancing in the direction of the horse barn, he shook his head. "Those cannot be the boots of Señor Vance. If he put the horses away, his tracks would come from over there."

"Maybe he rode."

The old man was adamant. "There are no hoof-prints."

Layla wrapped her arms around herself to contain a shiver. "Then who's in the house?"

"It could be one of the other men, looking for Señor Vance," Norberto said, studying the ground.

Layla watched him puzzle it out until the silence was so unbearable she had to ask, "What?"

"Look for yourself. A man went in. He did not come out."

"Maybe he used another door."

"That is possible. Wait here. I will go check."

Before Layla could stop him, Norberto had broken into a trot and disappeared around the west side of the ranch house, leaving her standing alone.

Never before had she noticed uneasiness because of being by herself. On the contrary, going solo had always given her peace. Now, however, she was *not* a happy camper.

The yard was empty. The surrounding countryside was quiet. Too quiet. It was as if the ranch itself was holding its breath.

Disgusted, Layla blew a cloud of condensation and gave herself a lecture. "This is silly. I'm a grown woman, not a little girl afraid of the dark. I'm not going to start imagining bogeymen in every dark corner just because somebody else is overly cautious."

She squared her shoulders and marched up the porch steps, insisting, "It's still daylight. Norberto's nearby. There's nothing to fear."

Her hand grasped the knob and turned it. As usual, the door was unlocked. A whoosh of warm, inviting air greeted her as she stepped inside, wrapping her in comforting feelings of home and hearth.

On a lark, she called out a cheery, "Honey, I'm home."

The sound of her inane greeting echoed through the silent rooms. Layla giggled to relieve anxiety. She was turning, intending to stick her head out the door and assure Norberto that she was fine, when someone or something smashed into her shoulder and knocked her against the door, slamming it closed.

Layla fell to her knees.

A viselike hand gripped her shoulder and threw her aside.

She screamed.

Before she could recover her senses enough to identify the intruder, a dark figure bolted past, jerked open the door and vanished.

Michael and Norberto arrived in the kitchen together. It was Michael who bent and pulled Layla to her feet. "What happened?"

"I—I don't know. Somebody knocked me down."

"Are you okay?" He sounded breathless.

As soon as she nodded, Michael turned his attention to his hired hand. "I told you to stay with her."

"It's not Norberto's fault," Layla quickly explained. "He told me to wait outside while he checked the front of the house but I..."

Michael's arm tightened around her shoulders, drew her closer. "You couldn't follow directions. Why am I not surprised?"

Again, he glared at Norberto. "What did you find?"

"Nothing, boss. No more tracks. I was coming to tell the *señorita* we should go to the barn and wait for you when I heard her yell." He spread his hands in a gesture of frustration. "*Lo siento*—I am sorry."

"I'm not blaming you," Michael said. "Go see to the horses. I got them both unsaddled but I hadn't had time to rub them down or feed them. I'll stay here."

Layla looked up. "What if there was more than one man?"

"Good point. Okay. Norberto and I will check the rest of the house before he leaves. Do you think you can stay put, for once?"

He didn't wait for Layla's answer before he took her hand and said, "Never mind. I know better. Just come with me. That way I won't have to wonder what else you've gotten yourself into."

"Hey, I couldn't help that there was a prowler in your house. What do you think he was after, anyway?"

"Beats me. He probably didn't think we'd come home so quickly. I'll check the safe in the den. Norberto, you check the bedrooms and closets in the back of the house."

"*Si*, boss."

Layla held back, tugging on Michael's hand. "Don't we need a weapon? Something to defend ourselves with?"

He raised an eyebrow. "A weapon? Last I heard, you didn't approve of such things. Have you changed your mind?"

"Maybe. Probably. I didn't enjoy being thrown around and trampled."

Pausing, Michael studied her expression. "You sure you're okay?"

"I'm fine. All I hurt was my pride."

"Which is considerable," he taunted. "Someday I'll have to try to teach you the difference between courage and idiocy."

"It's a pretty fine line." Layla was smiling.

Michael nodded as he led her down the hall by the hand. "For you, it probably is."

She had to take two steps for every one of his. "Oh, yeah? Well, I'm not the one poking around, looking for burglars, empty-handed."

"I'd rather you didn't announce that fact quite so loudly, just in case."

"Sorry."

"Besides, I thought you didn't believe in using violence to fight violence."

She made a face at him. "That was before I met you."

Layla was still with Michael when they finished the search and he dialed Sam Vance to report the latest development. To her relief and delight, Michael put the call on speakerphone and she heard Sam say, "I'll radio Becky Hilliard and ask her to stop by your place. She's already out that way."

"How about the local sheriff?" Michael asked.

"Right now, I think we should consider your prowler as part of our ongoing investigation. Besides, I want Becky to talk to your lady friend. Maybe she can get more out of her than I did."

Michael cleared his throat noisily. "Uh, Sam? Layla's here with me. We're both listening. I thought you knew."

Layla was pretty sure she heard a muffled expletive in the background. She giggled. "Hi, Detective. How's it going?"

"Not as well as I'd hoped," Sam said. "But since you're on the line, have you remembered anything else?"

"No." Layla sobered. "I really did tell you everything I knew the first time we talked. There's no hidden connection between me and the dead man. At least not that I'm aware of." She watched Michael's face, saw him nod support. "Maybe the collision was really an accident. Maybe the guy was just in a hurry and I was in his way."

"In his way?" Sam echoed. "I'd never thought of it quite like that before. What do you think, Mike? Has Dr. Dixon been getting in anybody's way?"

Thoughtful, Michael gazed at Layla. His brow knit. "In a manner of speaking. She's the one who figured out what was killing my cattle."

"That might be enough."

"I can't see why. Doc Pritchard never said anything about being threatened or attacked after he'd been here."

"He did leave town, though."

"Sure," Michael said, "but he was always talking about wanting to visit Las Vegas."

"Just the same, I think I'll see if I can track him down, make sure he's all right. There's always the chance he didn't leave Colorado Springs of his own free will."

Layla shivered.

Michael circled the desk and draped his arm around her shoulders. "Let us know as soon as you can, will you, Sam? Layla's looking kind of peaked. She'd never admit it, but I think you've scared her."

"Will do. Watch for Becky. She should get there in an hour or so."

"Fine," Michael replied. "Take care. And thanks, Sam."

Hanging up, Michael gave Layla's shoulders a squeeze of encouragement before releasing her.

"I'm confused," Layla said.

He arched an eyebrow. "What else is new?"

"I'm serious. I don't want to get off on the wrong foot with Detective Hilliard like I did with Sam. What should I call her? Rebecca, Becca or Becky?"

"Sam's the only one who ever slips and calls her Becky. It's a quirk of his. I think she prefers Becca."

"That's how she introduced herself to me," Layla said.

"There you go. Problem solved. Any other questions?"

Layla gave him a look that was a cross between silly and cynical.

He laughed. "Don't worry. You'll like Becca when you get to know her better. And I know she'll like you. She's real down-to-earth. Raised her brother and sister after their mother passed away."

Layla frowned. "When we were at church the other night, I thought Holly said Becca wasn't crazy about children."

"I suppose she feels she's already raised a family. She and Sam were an item, years ago, but he wanted a big family and she didn't. His wife, Jessica, already had Amy when she married Sam. They have a set of twins now, too."

Thoughtful, Layla walked away from him and stood by the window, staring into the icy yard. "Sam did the right thing. It's crucial for a husband and wife to agree on important points like that. Married life is hard enough without having to overcome hurdles that could have been avoided by discussing them in the first place."

"I agree." Michael's voice was low, compelling. "So, how do *you* feel about kids?"

Layla whirled. "Me? Why?"

He shrugged. "Just wondered. I'm not sure whether I'd make a good father or not. My dad was the best."

"If you love your children even half as much as

you do this ranch and your livestock, they'll turn out fine."

"Thanks." He smiled wryly. "Do you really think so?"

"I know so," Layla said. "I wish my parents…"

"What?"

"Never mind. It's just a hang-up I have. My folks raised me and my brother and sister to be independent. I like being that way. Sometimes, I wish Mom and Dad weren't quite so happy without me, that's all."

"Have you ever told them how you feel?"

Layla's head snapped around. She stared, scowled. "Of course not. Why would I do that?"

Shrugging, Michael smiled at her. "Oh, I don't know. Maybe to show them you still need their love, too."

"I don't," she insisted. "I'm fine just as I am. And I don't need lecturing, either."

"I wasn't—"

"Forget it."

Whirling, she headed for the kitchen so he wouldn't see the tears she was blinking back. The longer she hung around Michael Vance and the Double V, the more she realized how much she'd been missing.

It wasn't his fault he was a part of a big, loving family and a big, loving church, any more than it was her fault she wasn't. It was the stark contrast that hurt. That, and her inability to let go of her prejudices enough to step into the circle of joy his life represented.

He'd called her foolishly courageous. She wasn't

brave at all. If she had a speck of courage to spare, she'd use it to confess her feelings to her handsome boss and accept whatever he said in return, even if it broke her heart.

"Before I leave here, I will," Layla promised herself. "I'll tell him. I really will."

Reacting to the conversation with herself, she made a face. What she needed right now was Smokey. At least when she talked to the dog, no one could accuse her of being totally out of touch with reality.

That thought brought a smile, a thankful heart and a prayer. "I am grateful for my insight into animals, Lord. I just wish I understood the people in my life half as well."

Looking over her shoulder to make sure she was still all by herself, she added in a whisper, "Especially Michael Vance."

Becca joined Layla in the kitchen and helped prepare the green salad while they talked.

"You're sure you don't mind?" Layla asked.

"Not a bit. I get pretty tired of doing the same thing all day long. This is a welcome break."

"Boy, not for me. I hate to cook. I'll be thrilled when Imelda can come back to work."

"Really? Don't you want to stay?"

"I wouldn't mind being the ranch vet for a while longer. I just don't belong in a kitchen." She smiled. "Except to eat, of course. Would you like to join us for supper? We have plenty."

"Thanks, but no thanks," the detective said. "I have stacks of paperwork piling up at the office. That's the worst part about my job. I hate filling out forms."

"Is there much crime in Colorado Springs? It seems pretty peaceful."

"There aren't nearly as many problems since Max broke up the big drug cartel," Becca said. "I'm assigned to hostage negotiations. We don't get many of those calls, so in my spare time I help out wherever I'm needed."

"It doesn't bother you to work with Sam?" Layla immediately retracted the question. "Never mind. I shouldn't have asked. It's none of my business. Michael told me you and Sam had dated and it slipped out."

"I don't mind answering." A shake of her head set her long, brown ponytail in motion. "Sam's happy. That's all that counts. He and I were always wrong for each other. It just took us a long time to see that." She paused, smiled at her hostess. "So, how do you feel about Michael?"

Layla's cheeks flamed. "Michael? Why?"

"I figured turnabout was fair play. You don't have to answer if you don't want to. It's not an official question."

"Whew! That's a relief. Your partner already thinks I'm hiding something."

"Are you?"

Layla frowned, sobered. "No. I don't know why everybody seems to think I am. I never met the man who ran me off the road. I don't know anything about Michael's missing foreman. And I didn't poison his cattle or do away with the regular vet. Does that about cover it?"

Becca laughed heartily. "I'd say it does. And for what it's worth, I believe you." She peered at the pot Layla was stirring. "What is that stuff, anyway?"

"Tofu and tomato with Italian spices. I'm making spaghetti sauce."

Stifling a grin, the detective backed away. "Wow. Okay. Well, the salad's done. Guess I'll be going. Nice talking to you again."

"Coward," Layla teased. "This sauce is delicious. Here, taste it."

Becca waved her hands in front of her as if she were fending off a charging bull rather than a harmless cooking spoon. "I'll take your word for that, too."

She was nearly to the door when she hesitated. "You never did tell me what you think of Michael."

"If you knew that," Layla said, smiling, "you'd be way ahead of me. I have no idea."

Becca was still laughing softly as she waved goodbye and left.

Alone in the kitchen, Layla stirred both the pot and her thoughts. Clearly, Michael liked her. He'd said so. The problem wasn't with him, it belonged solely to her.

She'd been positive of what she wanted out of life until she'd met the attractive rancher. Was it time to seriously rethink those past conclusions? Or was it folly to dream of another kind of life—one that gave her the kind of roots she'd never had before?

Would it kill her to relinquish her independence? Would that eventually stifle her too much? Or would it allow her to be who and what she really wanted to be? The idea of becoming a wife and mother was scary, yet enticing.

Layla chuckled. "Whoa, girl. Get a grip. You don't even know if the man is that interested in you!"

Yes, I do, she answered, recalling their kiss. He wouldn't have kissed her that way unless he was more than merely flirting. She supposed the real question was his motives.

And mine, Layla added. Until she decided what her own goals were and faced them squarely, there was no use rehashing notions about Michael.

She turned the stove burner to simmer, laid aside the cooking spoon and closed her eyes. "Father, help? I don't know what to do. I don't even know what to think. I know You brought me here for a reason but I'm still confused. I thought it was to help Michael with his cattle. Is there more? Am I supposed to see something else?"

Peace and wisdom settled over and around her like a soft, warm blanket. Limiting God's grace was like telling the sun not to shine or the grass not to grow. There were so many more amazing possibilities and blessings within His realm, it was mind-boggling.

Layla sighed. "Okay, Lord. I get it. All I have to do is trust You and do my best, right? Well, I am. At least I think so. If I'm missing something, help me see it? Please?"

She was concentrating so heavily on her prayer she failed to hear the door open. When she opened her eyes, Michael was standing there with a puzzled look on his face.

Layla gave him an apologetic smile. "Sorry. I didn't hear you come in."

"No problem." He shucked off his coat and hung it on a peg by the door. "That smells like something Aunt Lidia would fix." His lips curled in a lopsided grin. "Is it too much to hope there are meatballs in it?"

"Way too much," Layla answered.

"Oh, well. I can always pretend."

An amusing, if revealing, response came to Layla's mind and remained unspoken. If anybody was good at pretending, it was *her*.

Chapter Thirteen

Days that had seemed to fly by at first, now dragged. Though Layla did her best to keep busy, she still had far too much time for introspection.

To her delight, Winona and Wilbur had developed into the perfect cow-calf pair. It was too cold to leave them outside all the time because they'd been spoiled by the luxury of residing in the barn, but they now had free access to an outdoor pen as well as their usual stall.

Every time Layla saw Wilbur, his explorations of the big, wide world made her laugh. Everything was exciting and new to the frisky, rusty red and white Hereford calf. He was like an awkward, long-legged puppy, investigating every inch of his domain and seldom slowing down except to eat or nap.

Thankfully, Winona was providing lots of milk for her little one and he was rapidly gaining weight. Layla had already managed to teach Wilbur to accept her presence and a bit of petting. Winona didn't act as if she minded sharing his upbringing, either. Given his zest for life and sense of adventure, Layla figured the poor cow was probably glad to have his attention diverted, even for short periods of time.

Having prepared and served lunch, Layla had the afternoon to herself. Her truck was still in the body shop in town. Michael had assured her the repair work was progressing as expected but had ignored her hints that he take her to see it in person. If she didn't know better, she'd think he was acting clueless on purpose.

She stepped out into the bright sunshine, took a deep breath and was immediately blessed by the purity of the mountain atmosphere. The air temperature was rising in spite of the traces of snow that remained. Unfortunately, the snowmelt had created more mud than Layla had encountered for ages, calling for boots instead of moccasins.

Picking her way across the yard she headed for the horse barn. If she took it slow, she and Fatima could enjoy another of their almost daily outings. Thankfully, Michael didn't insist on accompanying them as long as they stayed in sight of the main ranch buildings.

The stable was deserted. *Good*. Layla greeted the mare with a smile and presented a raw carrot on her flat palm. "Hello, Fatima. Look what I brought you, baby."

Layla chuckled as the mare's velvety lips quickly snatched it up. "Hey, that tickles."

She picked up a hoof pick and entered the stall. "Wanna go for a ride? Huh? Well, you have to let me clean your feet first." Layla gently touched the horse's front leg and ran her hand along it to the pastern. "Come on. Lift your foot. That's a good girl."

Bending over with her back to the mare's head, she presented a perfect target. Fatima obliged by lifting one foot, then turned her head and nudged Layla in the rear, knocking her off balance.

She staggered, recovered and laughed. "No, smarty. No more carrots for you till we get you saddled."

After cleaning all four hooves, Layla slipped a bridle on the mare and led her out of the stall. She'd just finished tightening the saddle girth when she heard a cow begin to bawl in the distance. Her heart sped. Had Michael's livestock been poisoned again?

The agonized, repetitive mooing frightened Fatima and she danced away when Layla tried to mount.

"Easy, girl," Layla cooed. "Easy. It's okay."

Swinging into the saddle, she rode the mare out of the barn, got her bearings in relation to the distressed animal and headed that direction.

Apparently, others had heard the frantic calling, too. Michael and Norberto met her at the barn where Winona and Wilbur were kept.

Michael was first in the door. Layla stayed aboard Fatima and rode around to the outside portion of Winona's pen, hoping she was wrong about the source of the anguish.

To her relief, Wilbur wasn't hurt or sick. He wasn't even there! Winona, however, was standing at the fence, staring into the distance and calling her missing calf as if her heart would break.

Frowning, Michael emerged from the inside stall. Seeing Layla, he skidded to a stop. "What's happened? Can you tell?"

She shifted on the mare's back and leaned to scan the ground. "No. There's no way Wilbur could have escaped without leaving tracks in this mud. Whatever he did, he didn't come this way."

"His mama sure thinks he did," Michael countered, shouting over Winona's continuing cries. "Look at her. She hasn't taken her eyes off that pasture."

"I know. But there aren't any cattle out there. If he'd gotten loose, he'd have either headed for other cows because he was curious or stayed near his mother."

"You could always ask her what happened," Michael suggested, tongue-in-cheek.

"Very funny. It doesn't work like that and you know it." Layla peered into the distance. "I'll ride out a little way and see if I can spot him or pick up his tracks. I won't go far."

Michael and Winona were hollering in unison when she spun Fatima in a tight circle, gave her a nudge and headed for open country.

Michael considered following Layla in one of the ranch trucks, then decided against it. If she left the road, there was no telling what kind of difficult terrain she'd get into. Besides, with all this mud and muck, even four-wheel drive might prove iffy. The only surefire method of travel was on horseback.

Norberto saddled the Appaloosa while Michael gathered extra gear. "I have a cell phone and the walkie-talkies," he told the ranch hand. "And an extra slicker. Can you think of anything else?"

"Rope?"

"No. The calf's still small. If we do find it, I'll just sling it over my saddle like any other dogie."

"It will be motherless like a dogie if you don't hurry," Norberto gibed. "That cow is about to holler herself to death."

"Yeah. Sounds like it, doesn't it?" He managed a smile for his old friend and trusted employee. "You hold down the fort. If I'm not back by dark, send a posse."

"You serious, boss?"

"Naw. I'm less worried about the calf than I am about our cow mumbler. Wilbur's probably sound asleep in a pile of hay somewhere while Layla's running around out there getting herself lost."

He swung effortlessly into the saddle and handed one of the walkie-talkies to Norberto. "Listen for me. I'll keep you posted as best I can. Radio me if that calf turns up."

"Sí. Vía con Dios."

"Thanks." Michael held the Appaloosa back momentarily. He appreciated the words, praying that God was with them all while they searched for the calf. "And tell Imelda I'm sick and tired of eating rabbit food. When I get back, I want a big, juicy steak with all the trimmings waiting for me."

"But, boss—"

"No buts. You and I both know she's been up and around for weeks. I'm not asking her to go back to cleaning, just cooking supper. Got that?"

Norberto began to grin. "Imelda has missed you, too."

"Not half as much as I've missed her."

Michael kicked the Appaloosa and headed across the yard to pick up Layla's trail. She'd be going slowly in order to check for the calf's tracks. Catching up to her should be relatively easy.

His gut knotted. The crazy woman had gotten under his skin so deeply he couldn't stop thinking about her, worrying about her. Would he be as concerned if there hadn't been suspected attempts on her life? Probably. It was as if he'd elected himself her protector and was stuck with the job whether he liked it or not.

He chuckled with self-deprecating humor. "One thing about it, life is never dull with Layla Dixon around."

Layla had been riding in an ever-widening arc, like a hunting dog casting back and forth to pick up a scent. She saw Michael making a beeline for her and reined in the mare.

"Anything?" he called as soon as he drew near.

She shook her head. "No. Nothing. Just tire tracks."

"What?" She could see him scowling beneath the brim of his hat.

"Tire tracks. Looks like somebody's been through here in the past few hours. You can see where they almost got stuck in the mud."

"Where? Show me."

Layla led the way with Michael following. "Here. See?"

"Yeah." He dismounted to check the ground more closely. "That's really odd."

"What is? It just looks like one of your ranch trucks passed by."

"Exactly. None of my hands were assigned to drive out here. I'd never send a truck under these conditions."

"Then what's going on?"

"Good question," Michael said. "You go back to the ranch and tell Norberto what we found. I'll follow these tracks, see where they go."

Layla huffed. "No way, cowboy. You may have given up on Wilbur but I haven't. I'm going to keep looking."

"You're supposed to be the expert in animal behavior. If you haven't found his trail by this time, you know he probably stayed near the barn."

"Winona didn't think so."

"No, she didn't, did she?" He swung back into the saddle and gathered up the reins. "Okay. Suppose the calf didn't wander off? Suppose somebody snatched him?"

"Why would they do that?"

"Beats me. Why have all the other weird things happened around here?"

"It's been pretty quiet lately. I was beginning to think the worst was over."

"Yeah, me, too." Michael regarded her soberly. "Now that I think about it, you and I should stick together. Ride with me to check out the tire tracks, then I'll come back with you and we'll look for Wilbur. How's that sound?"

"Okay, I guess." As she watched, Michael pulled a handheld radio from his pocket and called Norberto to advise him of their new quest.

Layla stared. "Hey. How come you told me I'd have to go back to the ranch to notify Norberto? Were you trying to get rid of me?"

"I was trying to keep you out of trouble," Michael insisted. "In your case, that seems to be impossible."

"Who made you my official guardian, anyway?"

"I don't know. Guess I was just in the wrong place at the wrong time." He wheeled the Appaloosa and kicked it into a canter.

Following, Layla denied her hurt feelings. "Fine. Be that way. I don't care. As soon as I get my truck back, I'm out of here. You won't have to bother about me much longer."

She had to urge the mare to keep up with the larger horse's long strides. Mud splattered from the Appaloosa's hooves, landing in splotches on Fatima's chest and neck. Layla reined to the side so she could ride parallel.

In profile, Michael's jaw jutted stubbornly, his

spine stiff. *Well, too bad.* He was the one who'd complained about their relationship, not her. The accident on the winding mountain road wasn't her fault. Neither was finding the rattlesnake in her bathroom. So what if she'd gotten caught up in his problems by coming to the Double V? It still wasn't her fault.

She thought about telling him exactly that, then decided against speaking her mind. No matter what she said at this point, he was liable to take it wrong. Besides, it shouldn't matter whether he was upset with her or not.

That was the crux of her problem. It *did* matter to her what Michael thought. It mattered a lot. And the longer she remained on his ranch, the worse it would get.

Though her quick, initial comeback had been the result of bruised ego, she realized she'd spoken the truth. She did need to leave. As soon as possible. If she stayed any longer she was going to be so head-over-heels in love with the obstinate man she might never get over it.

Ahead, Michael caught sight of the ranch truck. It was apparently abandoned in the shadow of the same rise that held the mine shaft they'd used for shelter.

Layla slowed her mare to match the Appaloosa's walking pace. "Is that the truck we're after?"

"Looks like it." He held out his arm, barring her way. "You wait here. I'll go check it out."

"Uh-uh," Layla said. "Where you go, I go."

He stifled the comment on the tip of his tongue and dismounted. "Have it your way."

They left the horses and approached the truck on foot. Michael removed his glove to touch the hood. "The motor's still warm."

"Which means I was right. The tracks were fresh."

"You were right." Scowling, he glanced her way and found her wandering off. "Where do you think you're going?"

"Over here. Look!"

Joining her, he saw a soggy, trampled area about eight feet in diameter. It was filled with footprints of either an adult deer or a calf the size of Wilbur. Parallel furrows showed that an animal had been dragged from there into the mine.

Layla stared. "Are you thinking what I'm thinking?"

"I hope not. Did you bring a flashlight?"

"No. How about you?"

"There should be one in the truck. Hang on. I'll go look."

He opened the passenger side door and rummaged in the glove compartment, then proudly announced, "Got it!"

When he turned, ready to escort Layla into the mine, she'd disappeared.

A quick assessment of the footprints she'd left behind told him exactly what had happened. As usual, she'd walked blithely into peril without the slightest concern for his orders to the contrary.

Furious, Michael ran into the dark tunnel after her. If they ever did anything together without experiencing a major crisis, he'd probably wonder what he'd overlooked!

Layla paused just inside the mine entrance to let her eyes adjust to the dimness. It was no surprise that whoever had taken Wilbur had had to drag the poor little guy into the shaft. Cattle were notorious for hating dark places. If they couldn't tell what was ahead, instinct forbade them to enter. It was a survival skill.

"And a good one," she whispered. A shiver snaked up her back beneath her sweater. Her self-preservation instincts were just as keen, except they were being overridden by the urge to mother and protect the innocent calf.

She started forward with a tentative, "Wilbur? Are you in here?"

In the distance, echoing off the rock and through the tunnels, came a weak, answering bleat.

"Wilbur!" Layla shouted. "Wilbur, where are you?"

The calf began to bawl. Layla's heart leaped. He was alive! Strong! And lost somewhere within the labyrinth.

"Good boy," she called. "Keep talking. I'll find you."

Feeling her way along the rough rock wall of the tunnel, she stepped cautiously. She sensed Michael moments before she saw the beam of his flashlight come from behind.

"Over here," she yelled. "Shine the light over here."

The circle of illumination passed over the pile of broken rock to her right and came to rest at her feet.

"Stop!" Michael ordered.

"No. Listen. Wilbur's just a little farther."

"No, he isn't. Sound bounces off these walls. He could be half a mile away."

"Don't be silly." She heard his boots crunching on the littered floor. Clearly, he was hurrying.

"Slow down," Layla yelled. "I'm fine. There's no reason to run."

That said, she took another step. Her heel slipped. Rocks clattered into a hidden abyss. Starting to lose her balance, she made a futile grab for the wall.

Instead of halting her slide, the effort propelled her, feetfirst, down an incline strewn with gravel left over from the mining operation.

By the time she reached the bottom she was surrounded by a cloud of dust and hoping her jeans had held up. The part of her covered by them was certainly protesting over the rough landing.

Layla was sitting at the bottom of the sloping shaft, counting her blessings and taking stock of her physical condition, when Michael shone the light on her.

"Are you hurt?"

Her first thought was to joke by asking him if he was getting tired of that question. Aware of the concern and anger in his tone, however, she squelched that thought and said, instead, "Fine. Just dirty."

Dusting off her hands, she noticed that her fall had broken the cord that held her beaded silver bracelets together. She felt her wrist and found the bangles missing. "Oh, no!"

"What?" Michael shouted.

Before Layla could reassure him, she heard a clatter behind her. Rocks the size of golf balls began raining down. The beam from the flashlight danced over the walls and ceiling of the shaft ahead in a dizzyingly erratic pattern. Her self-appointed guardian was joining her.

She struggled to get out of Michael's way and let him pass. A fresh cloud of dust nearly obliterated him when he finally came to a stop several yards farther down.

"I told you I was fine," Layla said. "Why do you insist I can't handle things without your help?"

"Because you can't." Michael got to his feet, brushed himself off, and held out his free hand. "Show me your wrist. Did you break it?"

She was glad he couldn't see her expression because she was so put out she knew it must show. "Of course not."

"Then why were you holding it?"

"I was checking my bracelets," she said flatly. "They broke. Shine the light on the floor for a second and I'll see if I can find the beads."

"Bracelets? This was about *bracelets?*"

"You don't have to yell. I told you I was fine. It's

not my fault you didn't take my word for it. I didn't ask you to come whooshing down here like a kid on a playground slide."

His lack of response told her more than she wanted to know about his mood. Instead of reaching for his hand, she clambered to her feet on her own and covered the last few feet to the tunnel floor where Michael now stood.

"If you're not going to help me find what's left of my jewelry, then let's go get Wilbur. That is what we came for."

"Maybe it's what you came for," he said, ire still coloring his speech. "I wouldn't be here if you hadn't been reckless enough to fall down a mine shaft."

"I didn't fall. I slid."

"Pardon me. You slid. That makes it all okay."

"It sure makes it better," Layla gibed. "Lighten up, okay? We're both down here and we're both unhurt, so we may as well go get the calf. Together. Unless you have something else to suggest."

"Would it do me any good?"

Layla laughed. "Nope. Come on. Let's go rescue Wilbur."

Michael led the way. He wasn't about to pass the flashlight to Layla and give her control of their pace. He'd explored these old shafts as a boy and knew plenty about the inherent dangers. Not only did the various mines run for miles beneath Cripple Creek and Colorado Springs, they were filled with twists and turns. Even if people didn't get lost, chances were good they'd come across vertical shafts that led to deeper and deeper grids of crosshatching, horizontal tunnels. It was no place for a novice.

"I still hear him mooing," Layla said, pulling on Michael's sleeve. "I think he's over here."

"No. This way."

"Are you sure?"

"More sure than you are." He shone the light into the niche she'd indicated to show her how shallow it was. "I've been in this mine before." To his surprise, she stopped arguing.

"Tell me more," Layla urged. "What's the layout?"

"Pretty basic. They tunneled horizontally till they ran out of rich deposits, then followed the silver veins as well as they could. That's why it sometimes seems like we're wandering."

She tugged on his coat again. "What about over here?"

"It's probably a dead end, just like the last one."

"But you're not sure? Show me."

Michael obliged. His jaw clenched. Leave it to Layla to point out one of the only passable tunnels besides the one they were in.

"I haven't explored down that way for years," he said. "It may have caved in. The shafts weren't all shored up as well as this one is."

Pausing, she called, "Wilbur? Where are you?"

The answering bleating echoed, sounding as if it came from all sides.

"We're never going to find him at this rate." She

snatched the flashlight out of Michael's hand and whirled, lighting the smaller arch of the side shaft as she hurried toward it.

He lunged after her. "Stop!"

Layla ignored him.

He had no choice but to follow and try to reclaim the light. Muttering under his breath, he gritted his teeth and forged ahead, using the reflected illumination to guide his steps. If she got too far away he'd be left in total darkness. And she'd be on her own. Neither outcome was acceptable.

The tunnel grayed. Layla had obviously turned a corner. Michael was about to call to her to slow down when he heard her cut loose with a shriek that stood his hair on end.

Layla froze. The body lying on the expanse of floor was grotesque. She stared. Someone had just screamed. Was it her? She was too numbed by the horrible sight to be certain.

Michael bolted into the cavern and skidded to a stop.

She waved the light at the object on the floor, her hand shaking. "Who…?"

He pushed past, bent down, then straightened slowly. "It's Ben. My missing foreman."

"But, how—why—?"

"Why is he so well-preserved after all this time? It's my guess the cold weather and dryness in the mine this time of year is responsible. I don't think his death is recent."

Again, Wilbur's bleating echoed. This time, when Layla swung the light in the direction of the sound, she spotted the calf.

Thankful for a more uplifting find, she left Michael and ran to the calf.

"Oh, Wilbur, honey. You poor thing. You must be starving. Who tied you up like this, huh?"

The Hereford butted her with his head, begging for food. Rather than take the chance of releasing him and having him bolt, she used the rope to fashion a makeshift halter and lead.

Turning back to Michael, she smiled. "He's okay."

"Good. Let me see that light. Over here."

Layla joined him with Wilbur in tow. "What is it? What did you find? Not another victim, I hope."

"In a manner of speaking." He took the flashlight and swung it in an arc that encompassed a pile of plastic jugs, then gave one of them a kick. It lightly bounced away. "See? They're empty."

"Antifreeze containers?" She was astounded. "What are those doing way down here?"

"They were obviously hidden," Michael answered. "The question is, did Ben do it or was he killed because he discovered what was going on?"

Layla shivered. "Let's get out of here."

"In a minute. I want to take some of these empty jugs to use as markers so I can find my way back here with Sam."

"Good idea. You carry those and I'll handle Wilbur. He's really hungry. I wouldn't want him to lick one of them and be accidentally poisoned."

"Okay." Michael filled his fists with jug handles. "You go first. I'll place these behind us as we walk out."

Layla started for the tunnel that had brought them there. Wilbur balked at entering the dark opening. She'd turned back and was tugging on his makeshift halter, urging him with softly spoken words, when Michael suddenly said, "Hush. Listen!"

"What?"

"I think I hear a motor."

Layla scowled. Her breathing increased. Her heart thudded so loudly she had trouble hearing anything else. "I'm not sure I do."

Suddenly, there was a flash.

The concussion of the blast blew her off her feet.

She stumbled over the calf and landed in Michael's open arms. They hit the ground. Hard.

Bits of rock were falling like sleet. Layla opened her eyes to a cloud of dust so thick she could barely see. She blinked to get her bearings. Her ears were buzzing. Her head throbbed.

Michael had cushioned her landing and saved her from serious injury. She stared at his expressionless face and felt her heart leap into her throat.

"Michael? Michael, speak to me!"

No answer came. He was unconscious.

Chapter Fourteen

Norberto was in the main house, helping Imelda prepare Michael's special dinner, when he heard King and Molly barking excitedly. He peered out the window.

"What is it," his wife asked.

"The horses!" Shouting, he straight-armed the door and paused in the opening. "Call 911! Get a rescue squad out here."

"Why? What has happened?"

Norberto grabbed the two-way radio. "Señor Vance? Señor Vance, answer me!"

He shook his head. "It is no use. Do as I told you. And have them tell Sam Vance what has happened, too. He will want to be here."

"Where are you going? What will you do?" Imelda hobbled to the door as her husband dashed for the barn.

"I don't know." Norberto was shouting for Hector and the other ranch hands as he ran.

Entering the stable, he found both horses lathered with sweat, their sides heaving as if they'd been running at breakneck speed. They blew condensation into the icy air, reminding Norberto that another frigid night was fast approaching.

He checked the saddles, thankful to find no sign that either rider had been injured. So what had unseated them? And where were they now?

Crossing himself, he sent up a silent prayer for Michael and Layla's safety, then picked up the telephone extension in the barn and buzzed the house.

Imelda answered immediately. "I called the police. Have you found anything?"

"No. Go look on Mr. Vance's desk and get me Detective Sam's private number. Hurry."

In what seemed like an eternity, Imelda was back on the line. She read her husband the number, then hung up.

He dialed. An answering machine took the call.

Frustrated and panicky, Norberto had to force himself to speak English. "Detective. Something *muy malo*—bad—has happened to my boss, Señor Michael. You must come. Bring a search…you know what I mean. The dogs. Bring the dogs. Get Julianna Red Feather. She will know what to do. Her dog, Angel, can find anyone. Hurry!"

When he hung up and turned, three other ranch hands were standing there, waiting to hear more. By the time Norberto had explained about the horses returning without riders, Hector had joined the group.

"I'll take over," Hector said. "As foreman, it's my

duty." He nodded at Norberto and the others. "You men finish cooling down the horses, then go back to your regular chores."

"What about following the tracks?" Norberto asked.

"If anyone goes out looking before the police arrive, it will be me," Hector answered flatly. "If you want to be useful, drive to the highway and flag down the rescue truck so it doesn't go past. We want it here as soon as possible."

Norberto's jaw clenched. So did his fists, but he reluctantly obeyed. If anything happened to his boss or the kind lady vet because of those stupid orders, he'd beat Hector to a pulp.

In the meantime, he'd pray harder than he had since Imelda gave birth to their daughter, Mercedes, twenty-five years ago.

Layla levered herself into a kneeling position and stared down at Michael, hoping and praying his injury wasn't serious. His chest moved. He coughed. He was breathing! *Thank You, God.*

Trying not to jostle him, she edged to one side and gently stroked his cheek. Since there was a chance of a spinal cord injury, he shouldn't be allowed to move once he regained consciousness. *If* he did.

That thought pierced her like a knife. Michael had to be all right. He *had* to be. What would she do without him?

Tears dropped from her cheeks onto his. She

blotted them with the cuff of her sweater, using the moisture to help clean off the worst of the dust coating his eyelids. They fluttered.

"Michael?" she whispered.

He blinked. "What...?"

"There was an explosion," Layla said. She used both hands on his shoulders to keep him from rising. "Lie still. You might have a head or back injury. You mustn't move till we're sure."

To her relief, he relaxed beneath her ministering touch and brought one hand to his forehead. "It must have been a lulu. I don't remember a thing."

"All I know is, there was a really bright flash and a bang. It knocked me into you and we both went down. I'm afraid that's why you hit the ground so hard."

Michael winced and smiled at the same time. "Better me than you. Are you okay?"

"Yes." She sniffled. "I feel much better now that you're conscious."

He reached for her face, cradling her damp cheek. "Are you crying?"

"Maybe." She sniffled again and wiped her eyes on her sleeve. "I was afraid I'd lost you."

"You care that much?"

Layla nodded.

Threading his fingers through her tousled, dusty hair he drew her face closer before he said, "I love you, too, Doc. I guess I have for a long time."

Speechless, she answered the only way she could. She bent and kissed him.

* * *

Norberto had sent one of the younger men to wait by the road and had stationed himself near the barn, planning to be included in the rescue team no matter what.

He was overjoyed to see his prayers had been answered. Julianna Red Feather was there and had brought her famous search dog. Angel was a German shepherd with an amazing reputation for finding victims of disasters, but Julianna had burned out on the job last year. It was good to see she wasn't letting her personal feelings keep her from helping. At least not this time.

Pumping her hand, Norberto said, "Bless you, *señorita*. I know you will find them."

The petite, half-Pueblo swung her long, black braids behind her, laid her hand on the dog's head and smiled sadly. "I'll do my best. You know I can't promise that Angel and I will succeed."

"I know." Norberto nodded. "Like I told Detective Sam, Señor Michael and Señorita Layla went looking for a lost calf. The cow is still crying for her little one. If we let her out and follow her, she can lead us in the right direction."

Julianna frowned thoughtfully. "I don't know. That could muddy up the tracks and confuse the scent trail. Tell you what. Why don't you let Angel get her bearings first? Then, if she strikes out, we'll try it your way."

Norberto choked up. *"Gracias, señorita."*

"You're quite welcome."

All business, the dog handler turned her attention to Sam Vance. "I'll need a sample of something the missing people wore recently. I want to see the saddles and horses, too. We're asking a lot of Angel if they've traveled a long distance."

"All of that's waiting for you in the barn," Sam said. "Judging by the deep hoofprints they left, those horses were really spooked. Looks like they were running full-out, scared to death, headed straight for home. It should be a pretty easy trail to backtrack."

"Then let's get started," Julianna said, setting her jaw and standing as tall as her five-foot-three-inch height would allow. "This time, I intend to get to the victims before it's too late."

Layla had finally satisfied herself that Michael wasn't badly hurt and had allowed him to get up. His pupils were equal and reactive, meaning he probably didn't have a concussion, and she could find no visible injuries except a small cut on his scalp.

Once she was sure the man she loved was all right, she checked Wilbur. The poor little calf was shaking and seemed stunned, but all in all, the three of them had made it through the explosion in remarkably good shape.

Michael shone the light on the blocked exit as he picked his way across the rock-littered floor. "I have a bad feeling about this."

"There must be another way out. You said these hills were riddled with tunnels."

"Not necessarily interconnected ones. There are

lots of dead ends, places where they lost the vein, dug around till they had a cavern like this one, then gave up and went back to start over."

Layla tried to hide her shivering. Michael had enough to worry him. She wasn't about to let on how frightened she was and add to his concerns.

"Okay," she said. "What now?"

"Beats me. I guess we try to dig our way out."

"Looks like that might take a long time."

"True." He slipped his arm around her and gave her a brief hug before placing a kiss on her temple. "Umm. Gritty. Just the way I like my women."

She knew he was trying to lift her spirits and played along. "Thanks bunches. You're not exactly ready for the Broadmoor, either, cowboy."

"*Now* you tell me." Handing her the light, he said, "Shine that on the slide. I'll get started."

"I'm going to help."

"Then prop it on a rock or something and let's get to work. I'm not sure how long those batteries will last."

Layla knew exactly what he meant. She'd had the same morbid thought. For now, they had light to work by and air to breathe. Sooner or later, they'd run out of both.

Laying aside the flashlight, she rejoined Michael and began to attack the loose rock. Jagged edges tore at her fingers. Dust filled her throat, made her eyes water, her head ache even more than before.

The pile blocking their way seemed never-ending. No sooner did they remove some of the loose face than more slid forward to take its place.

"Are we getting anywhere?" Layla asked.

"We'd better be. I don't intend to stay stuck in here when you and I have such a wonderful future ahead of us."

"You meant it? You love me?"

"Of course I did. Have I ever lied to you?"

"No."

She bent her head, letting her loose curls drop beside her cheeks to hide new tears that insisted on being shed. It wasn't fair. She and Michael had just discovered their mutual love. They couldn't lose that.

"I love you, too," she said quietly. "So much I can't even tell you."

"Then save it for later, when we're safe and sound."

A tender, poignant vow came to mind. Layla kept it to herself rather than trust her voice.

I will love you, Michael Vance, for the rest of my life. She tried to swallow past the lump in her throat. *Till death do us part. Even if that's only a few hours away.*

Julianna's dog had lost the scent of the humans she was tracking soon after they'd left the barn area. While the others followed the horse's hoofprints on foot and aboard four-wheel-drive ATVs, she piled into a truck with Norberto. Angel sat between them, eager as ever.

"Take it slow," she cautioned. "Make sure we don't get sidetracked because we're in too big a hurry."

He was leaning out the driver's window. "I can see the trail. We will find them."

"What do you think happened?"

"I do not know. We have much trouble here. Señor Sam has been investigating."

"Really? Investigating what?"

Norberto filled her in on the details as they drove, then suddenly slammed on the brakes.

"What is it?"

"Here. This is where the horses were when they started to run!" He stared at the disturbed ground, then triggered his walkie-talkie. "Señor Vance? Doctor? Can you hear me?"

The radio crackled, sounding like someone was frying bacon instead of responding. Norberto leaned on the truck's horn; three long bursts, three short, three long, three short.

"SOS." Julianna grinned. "Okay. C'mon, Angel. Here's where you go to work!"

Inside the mine, Layla and Michael had worked to near exhaustion. She knew they'd been pumped up by an initial surge of adrenaline that was now dissipating. She also knew that although they should have been tired from their hard labor, there was more to their current fatigue than that. They must be running low on oxygen.

Michael had shed his jacket. Clearly, he was forcing himself to go on when his muscles were screaming for rest. Hers certainly were.

"Stop," Layla said, reaching to clasp his hand and still it. "That's enough. Rest."

"No!"

"Michael. Look at me. Please? The light's fading.

The batteries are almost dead. I don't want to spend our last hours together fighting with you."

Tears glistened, unshed. His shoulders sagged. "I won't give up. I can't. We'll get out of here."

"And if we don't?"

"Don't talk like that." He grasped both her hands and gazed into her eyes. "God won't let us die."

"I hope you're right. Then again, who are we that we should be given more second chances than anyone else?"

He set his jaw and didn't answer, so she went on. "I used to pray for things all the time when I was a child. When I didn't get answers, like a kid with a wish list of expensive toys and a rich daddy, I thought God wasn't listening to me."

"Now you think He was?"

"Yes. If I'd been raised differently, if my parents had been able to give me everything I'd asked for, I might never have become the person I am today." She smiled sweetly. "I might never have met you. Never have discovered where I belonged."

He pulled her closer and she rested her cheek on his chest, listening to the solid beating of his heart.

"I do belong here with you," Layla said quietly. "Believe me, I'm *not* ready to give up and die. I just want you to rest a little. To hold me like this."

"Without a chaperone?"

She raised her face to him and smiled. "We have Wilbur. He's taking a nap but I think he still counts."

"You're amazing, you know that?"

"Uh-huh. About time you realized." Ignoring the

grime they were both covered with, she slipped her arms around Michael's waist and gave him a squeeze before letting go. "Okay, cowboy. That's enough R & R. Back to work."

Michael smiled condescendingly. "All right. You can be the boss for once. Just don't get too used to giving orders." He sobered. "You might want to pray more while you're at it, too."

"More? I haven't stopped praying since somebody tried to blow us up."

To her delight and comfort, Michael nodded and said, "Neither have I."

"It's through here," Julianna called. "Follow us. Angel has the scent!"

Norberto was trailing them with an additional spotlight. He played it over the pile of rock blocking the tunnel ahead. "Are you sure?"

"Angel is. That's good enough for me."

The eager dog had started to whine and dig at the base of the slide. Julianna restrained her. "Easy, baby. You've done your part. We'll get them out for you."

Trying to inform the other searchers of their find, Norberto discovered that his cell phone was useless inside the mine.

He dashed outside to make the call. "We found them! The horses led us this far and the dog did the rest. Follow my tire tracks. And be careful when you leave the road. I almost got stuck."

In seconds he'd returned to Julianna. "I'm not going to wait. Start digging."

"With what?" She scowled at him.

"Hands." He was already flinging stones the size of concrete blocks out of the way.

"There's a shovel in the truck. I'll get it and help you," she said. "C'mon, Angel."

The German shepherd dug in her claws, crouched by the wall of loose rock and began barking frantically in spite of Julianna's tugging on her harness.

"Angel. What's gotten into you?"

Norberto held up his hand. "Hush. Listen. Do you hear something?"

"Only barking." She managed to quiet her dog long enough to gain a few seconds' peace. "Maybe. Was that a voice?"

"I think so." Norberto renewed his efforts. "I left the phone in the truck. Tell the rescue party to hurry!"

Layla was so exhausted she was imagining things. Considering the way every little sound echoed inside the sealed chamber, it wasn't surprising that her ears were playing tricks on her. First, she'd imagined the far-off tooting of a horn and now she was almost convinced she could hear talking. No wonder. Not only was there still a buzz in her head from the explosion, whenever Michael tossed aside another boulder it seemed to make the very walls of their prison vibrate.

Michael sank to his knees. Layla knelt beside him. She thought he might be praying until he asked, "Do you hear something?"

She listened. "No. I thought I did, but…"

"I thought so, too."

Layla gently touched his forearm. "It's okay." The gesture was meant to comfort, not upset him.

He froze. Shook her off. Held up his hand. "Shush."

"Why? I don't hear a thing."

"I don't either, now."

"Well you don't have to grumble at me. It's not my fault. I…" She was silenced by Michael's unexpected kiss.

Her pulse hammered in her ears. She shivered in spite of his warm embrace. Maybe fear and exhaustion had unhinged his mind and destroyed his grip on reality. He certainly wasn't behaving as sanely as he had been.

Nevertheless, Layla embraced him with all the love in her heart, willing him to accept the truth of her devotion. They might not be granted years in which to express their love, to grow in understanding and deepen their ties the way other couples did. If these few minutes or hours were all that remained, she couldn't deny Michael the kisses he wanted.

Suddenly, her whirling thoughts broke away from the moment at hand and zeroed in on something else. Something in the distance. It sounded as if mice were scratching on the other side of the rock slide!

Her eyes flew open, met Michael's knowing gaze.

He eased his hold and nodded. "*Now* do you hear it?"

"Yes!" Layla squealed in delight. To the slide she shouted, "Help! We're in here. Help!"

A muffled answer was punctuated by the barking

of a dog. Layla grabbed Michael's hand. "You're not crazy!"

He managed a chuckle. "I sure hope not. It sounds like we're going to be rescued."

El Jefe stood back and grinned. His enemies had walked right into his trap, like the fools they were. It was a fitting end for Michael Vance and his pretty vet. The only thing that would have been more to his liking was the opportunity to actually watch them die. To see the looks on their faces when he stood over them and they breathed their last.

He reached for his phone and punched in a familiar number. This was too precious a moment to keep to himself. He had to share the victory, to let his closest cohort know how clever he'd been once again.

The moment he heard, "Hello," he began to relate the details of his latest triumph.

"I have done away with Vance and the woman," he said. "They died knowing about that idiot Ben, the foreman I killed, and the poison. It was a brilliant ending."

"What will you do now?"

"Move on," *El Jefe* said. "There are many more of my enemies to tend to."

"But they will suspect."

"Not if I plan carefully and leave the right clues." He paused to chuckle with conceit. "Vance's first foreman disappeared without a trace. The second can easily fall victim to the same fate. So can any of his ranch hands. No one will suspect me."

"I thought you said Vance and the woman had found the foreman's body in the mine."

El Jefe laughed again, this time with more gusto. "They found the body all right. And they were buried with it. I saw to that. With Michael Vance gone and no one ready to take his place, the Double V will either fail or be sold. Either way, I win."

"Where will you go?"

"Into hiding, for the time being. I can operate out of the same tunnels we use to smuggle the drugs. If I have needs, you can supply them."

The sputtered answer on the other end of the line disgusted him. He broke the connection and slipped the phone back into his pocket. No one truly understood a superior intellect like his. They were all fools. He tolerated them only because they were necessary, not because he intended to honor his promises. Let them complain. He didn't care. He answered to no one but himself. Not even God could touch him.

Turning away, he started for the Double V. There was work to do. Loose ends to tie up. Clues to plant. The place was practically deserted, thanks to the useless rescue efforts that had drawn everyone into the hills. He'd never have a better opportunity than he had right now.

Norberto's hands were raw and bleeding. He'd dug until the rescue unit arrived. Then, fatigue had overcome him and he'd allowed himself to be helped from the mine and properly cared for.

A portable generator had been set up at the

entrance to provide light. An air compressor was already pumping oxygen to the trapped victims via a pipe that had been driven through the thinnest portion of the slide, near the tunnel roof.

"They'll be all right. You'll see," Julianna told him. "It's just a matter of time now."

Norberto had the strength to do little more than nod as a medic bandaged his hands and eased his pain.

Finally, he spoke to the young, dark-haired woman who had been the answer to his prayers. "Thank you for coming. I know it is hard for you."

"Yes," she said. "Very hard."

"But still you do it. That is a gift."

"I suppose you could say that. Angel's the one with the gift, though. Sometimes I think it's as hard on her to be too late to save someone as it is on me. When we lose a victim she mopes for days, like she's failed."

"Ah," Norberto said softly, "I see. But you are wiser. You know it is not in your hands."

"But it is."

"No. Your job is to do your best. To do what you have been trained for. The rest we must leave to God."

Chapter Fifteen

Michael heard the rescue workers clearly when one of them shouted, "Stand clear. We're about to break through."

He stepped beside Layla and put his arm around her when he saw she was shivering. "Know what I'm going to do first when we get out of here?"

"Take a shower?"

"After that," he said with a low chuckle.

"No. What?"

"Buy you a decent jacket. Preferably one with sleeves."

"My vest is comfortable."

"Fine. You can wear it when you're working with animals. The rest of the time, I want you to have a coat that actually keeps all of you warm."

"Picky, picky, picky." She smiled. "Are you going to let me have my truck back pretty soon, too? I miss having wheels."

"You think I've kept your truck from you?"

"Probably." Her smile widened. "And I forgive you. After all, if I hadn't stayed around we wouldn't have gotten stuck in here together and finally admitted how we felt."

Michael's grip tightened into a hug. "True. A lot has happened in a very short time. If you change your mind after you've had time to think about it, I'll understand."

"Oh, no. If you expect me to grant you the same concession, you have another think coming," Layla said, slipping her arms around his waist. "I don't plan on changing anything, especially not the way I feel about you, so you'd better get used to having me around."

"Yes, ma'am. Like I said before, it'll be my pleasure."

Above them, the rocks at the top of the pile began to move. Bright light flooded the cavern.

A rescue worker in a yellow helmet poked his head in. "You folks all right?"

"Never better," Michael said, shielding Layla with his body to protect her from any falling rocks. "We're sure glad to see you guys."

"Same here," the man said. "We've got an ambulance standing by. Have you out of there in two shakes of a calf's tail."

"Speaking of calves," Layla called, peeking around Michael, "we have a little one trapped in here with us. Can you take him out first?"

"Better do as the doc says and keep her happy,"

Michael added. "If she gets mad she's liable to make us all eat vegetables."

He and Layla were already smiling as the rescuer retreated. When they heard him tell his fellow team members, "You're not going to believe this," they burst into gales of laughter.

Layla giggled and chortled until tears ran down her face, streaking the dust.

Michael wiped his eyes. "I think we're overreacting."

She nodded, gasping for breath. "Probably. I get silly when I'm overtired."

"No doubt you're relieved, too."

"Boy, that's the truth." She managed to regain control of her emotions. "I'm glad it wasn't our time to go."

"Yeah. Me, too. I'm definitely not ready." He drew her closer. "You and I have a lot of living to do. Together."

"I think it would be wise to give ourselves a little time to get over all this trauma before we make any definite plans, don't you? We've been through a lot."

"We sure have. It'll probably take weeks to get all the dust out of our hair, let alone heal what we did to our hands trying to dig our way out of here."

"I still wouldn't trade a minute of it," Layla said. "It was exactly what we needed."

Michael agreed. He didn't believe the cave-in had been divine intervention but things had turned out for the best anyway. Whoever had set off the explosives, thinking to end their lives, had inadvertently given them a new start.

No doubt Pastor Gabriel would imagine the Lord's hand in the disaster, Michael mused, in spite of their ending up trapped by it. He disagreed until he remembered the way the calf had balked and delayed Layla's intended progress toward the main tunnel.

His mouth went dry, his breath caught, his gut tied in a knot as hefty as one of those boulders.

If Layla hadn't been so concerned for Wilbur's feelings she would have been buried by tons of loose rock. And he'd have been right beside her.

It didn't take a theologian to recognize a beneficial, even providential, act when he saw it.

Wilbur had been reunited with his unhappy mama and had nursed, to Winona's great relief. By the time Layla and Michael got cleaned up and met with the police in the kitchen of the main house, everything was back to normal. Smokey and Molly were snoozing beneath the table and King lay at his master's feet.

Norberto and Imelda had gone home but the capable cook had prepared enough food for a small army so Michael insisted Sam and Becca stay for supper. He had more than the detectives' well-being in mind, however. He wanted to stay close to Layla, no matter what, and was using the others as a convenient buffer.

"I should be getting home." Sam pushed away

from the table. "Jessi will worry. I try to always be there to tuck in Amy and the twins." He smiled proudly. "Guess I've spoiled them."

"Have some dessert first," Michael urged. "Imelda's cakes are delicious."

Sam patted his stomach. "No, thanks. I'm stuffed. But I will let you send some home with me."

"Done." Michael jumped up and brought the cake to the table with a flourish.

Layla and Becca exchanged glances. Layla's eyebrows arched. "I don't know how you do it, cowboy. I'm so sore I can hardly move and you're running around like a chicken with its head cut off." The analogy made her wince. "Sorry. Poor choice of words."

Becca chuckled. "I hate to tell you this, Layla, but there was meat in the enchiladas."

"Not in mine," she replied "I got the plain cheese ones. Somebody must have told Imelda about my funny eating habits."

Smiling, Michael nodded. "I may have mentioned it. She was supposed to fix me a steak. I guess she changed the menu when we were so late getting home."

"Yeah," Sam said. "It's a wonder you got here at all. By the way, did I tell you we located Doc Pritchard? He's vacationing in Las Vegas, just like we thought."

"That's a relief. I was afraid he was another victim of whatever's been going on around here."

"So was I," Sam said. "Sure you haven't got a clue who could have set off the explosion?"

"Nope, no idea," Michael said. "When the medical examiner gets through with Ben's body, maybe that report will tell you something, although I doubt it." He looked at Layla while continuing to speak to Sam. "It might have been an accident. You know how unstable old dynamite can be. Maybe some of it went off spontaneously."

"And maybe pigs can fly," the detective said.

That made Layla giggle. "I hope not. Little birds in the sky are bad enough!"

While the laughter died down, she yawned. "I'm sorry, guys. I'm exhausted. If you don't have any more questions for me, I think I'll wander home. Try to get some sleep."

"Don't go!" Michael's response was so quick it startled everyone, including himself.

Layla reached for his bandaged hand, saw him wince when she touched him and drew back. "I'll be fine. Honest. You know I can't stay here with you."

"If it's a chaperone you need, I'll be glad to volunteer," Becca said cheerfully. "You two have been through a lot today. It's perfectly natural for you to want to stay together a while longer." She turned to Sam. "Go home, partner. Kiss your kids for me. I'll either hitch a ride into town tomorrow or you can come back and pick me up. Either way's fine."

"You serious?"

"Totally."

"Okay." Sam rose. "I'll get some cake tomorrow, then. 'Night everyone."

Michael walked him to the door while Layla stayed behind with Becca.

* * *

As soon as they were outside where the women couldn't overhear, Sam stopped, looked around to make sure they were totally alone and spoke quietly. "There's something that still puzzles me. Something that's not quite right."

Michael's brow knit. "Like what?"

"I don't know. Blaming everything on a dead man seems too easy, too pat." He paused, thoughtful. "We'll have to wait for the coroner's final report but I suspect your old foreman has been dead a long time."

"Probably. Why is that a problem?"

"Because, if he was already out of the picture, who poisoned your cattle? And while we're at it, who blew up that mine tunnel while you were inside? I'm pretty sure we're going to find it was no accident."

"I told Layla I thought some old dynamite might have gone off spontaneously. That stuff can be pretty unstable."

"True. But dynamite doesn't reposition itself to take out the only tunnel that might kill people."

"Good point." Glancing back at the house, Michael was obviously growing as concerned as Sam. "Once I'd decided the antifreeze in the feed wasn't an accident, I assumed Redding was responsible. Now that I think about it, though, I suppose it could have been someone else."

Sam proceeded to his car, then turned and faced Michael. "It sure could have. Somebody on the inside, maybe. What about Hector? He showed up here just when you needed a foreman. He was either lucky enough to be in the right place at the right time or he knew in advance that you were going to be shorthanded."

"He never acted suspicious." Michael stiffened. "Do you think he might have killed his predecessor just to get his job? That seems awfully far-fetched."

"Nothing criminals do surprises me anymore. I'm going to suggest that Brendan have the FBI look deeper into Hector's background. It can't hurt."

"Sure. Whatever you think will help. I haven't seen him since we got home but he's probably in the barn. Do you want me to call down there or go get him so you can question him tonight?"

"No. You've had a rough day. We're all beat. There's no hurry. Just keep your doors locked and watch yourself." Sam smiled. "And keep an eye on that pretty vet, too."

"Now you're on the right track," Michael said, smiling. "That's a job I can do gladly."

Inside, Layla was expressing relief that Becca had volunteered to stay the night. "Thanks. I really didn't want to leave Michael or be by myself, but I didn't know what else to do."

"I figured as much." Becca began carrying dishes to the sink and rinsing them. "I'll take care of this for you. You shouldn't get your sore hands wet. Why don't you go crash on the sofa in the living room? I'll tell Mike where to find you when he comes back inside."

"I like Michael's friends," Layla said, pausing halfway to the hall door. "You're all very special people."

"So are you. I get the feeling you and our favorite rancher have come to an understanding. Am I right?"

He walked back into the room in time to answer, "Yes," for both of them, then strode directly to Layla and put his arm around her shoulders.

She leaned into him. "Um-hum. Does it show?"

"Sam may have missed it, but that's because he's a man. For me it's like a flashing neon sign," the female detective said with a chuckle. "Now scat, you two. I've got plenty to keep me busy here and you both need to kick back. I'll join you in a few minutes."

"You're sure you don't mind?" Layla asked.

"Nope. Go, before I get all misty-eyed. You guys look way too happy to suit me and it's not good for cops to get overly sentimental. Ruins our hard-boiled image."

Smiling and still guarding Layla as if he planned to do so for the rest of their lives, Michael led her from the kitchen into the living room.

She curled her legs under her as she sat beside him on the smooth leather couch. She snuggled closer. "I could get used to this."

"Yeah, me, too," he said tenderly. "Think we can talk Becca into moving in to chaperone us for the next few months?"

Layla laughed. "I doubt it."

"Too bad. I'd like to spend every night with you, just like this."

"I know. Me, too." She sighed and smiled dreamily. "I wish we didn't both know it was wrong."

"It's more than that," Michael said. "I respect you, Layla. I intend to take care of you, to keep you safe no matter what, but I never want to do anything that would make people think less of you, either." He leaned in to place a light kiss on the top of her head. "We can wait. Somehow." He laughed softly. "Even if it kills me."

"You poor thing." She blushed. "I know we agreed not to rush into anything but I don't want to wait *too* long. I've looked all my life for a place where I can truly belong. Now that I've finally found it, I don't want to take the chance of losing it."

"You'll never lose me, I promise. There's nothing you could do or say that would make me stop loving you."

"I love you, too, cowboy."

Layla's eyes were filled with tears of thankfulness, love and divinely inspired awareness as she raised her face to accept his kiss. The past was over. The future was bright. And she was finally going to become part of a real family, a family that would love and accept her just as she was.

She knew how Michael felt. She could hardly wait.

Epilogue

El Jefe stormed into the dimly lit room, kicked the door shut behind him and proceeded to pace.

He repeatedly slammed his fist into his opposite palm like a baseball hitting a catcher's mitt. "I don't believe it! It can't be."

His companion remained in the shadows and let him rant rather than face his wrath directly.

"How can they have escaped?" *El Jefe* shouted. "They should be dead. They must all die. It is my due, my just payment for what the Vance and Montgomery families did to me."

"Perhaps—"

"Quiet! Let me think." He whirled, then pulled a cigarette from the pack in his shirt pocket. "I should have shot those horses first," he muttered. "Their tracks led the rescuers straight to the mine."

"The explosion still might have killed Vance and the woman."

"I know. I don't understand how it missed."

While his cohort watched, he seemed to suddenly grow calm. Taking out a match, he struck it on the edge of the table, held it up and watched it burn instead of using it to light his cigarette.

As he stared into the flame his demeanor changed again and became so menacing it sent a shiver of terror through his companion.

The flickering match lit the stark planes of his face and reflected from his dark eyes, revealing flashes of pure evil. He began to quote from the Bible, abridging and altering the text to suit his madness.

"Kings 1:10," he boomed. "'If I am a man of God, then let fire come down from heaven and consume you all!'"

Laughing low, as if to himself, he added Hebrews 12:29. "'For our God is a consuming fire.'"

That passage of Scripture seemed to amuse him even more. He faced his cohort and grinned with evident self-satisfaction. "Yes!"

"I don't understand."

"You soon will," *El Jefe* said. "You soon will. And so will my enemies. I know what to do. We begin."

"Begin what?"

Eyes wide and overly bright, *El Jefe* stared at the roof of the hidden room as if seeing through the rock to the surface.

"Begin proving to Colorado Springs that I am truly invincible."

"Now? So soon after the explosion at the Double V? Are you sure?"

There was no hesitancy. "Yes. It's time."

* * * * *

Dear Reader,

If you're familiar with my other books, you'll notice that this one is a bit different. Six authors were asked to participate in a series set in Colorado and I was thrilled to be included.

Many thanks to my fellow authors, Lois, Sharon, Marta, Terri and Margaret, and to our editor, Diane, of course. We brainstormed via e-mail and worked hard to make our series books fit together, as well as be wonderful stand-alone tales of love, faith and romantic suspense.

I also want to thank my other Colorado friends, Vicki and Carol, for answering my questions about daily life in the shadow of the Rockies.

Although I'm very particular about details in my books, I also understand that being a joyful believer is not dependent upon location or circumstance. Rather, it is a condition of the heart. Peace is found in Christ, no matter where life takes you. If that peace and sense of belonging is missing, it won't be found by running away or by traveling aimlessly, as Layla learns in this story. To belong to God's family, all you have to do is turn to Jesus and humbly ask for forgiveness. His arms are always open to embrace you.

I love to hear from readers. The quickest replies are by e-mail—valw@centurytel.net—or you can write to me at P.O. Box 13, Glencoe, AR, 72539 and I'll do my best to answer as soon as I can. Or visit my Web site: www.centurytel.net/valeriewhisenand/

Blessings,

Valerie Hansen

The heat is on! Firefighter Lucia Vance has been worried about her father, who'd been shot in an assassination attempt months earlier. And now it seems that someone wants Lucia out of the way. Good thing for her that smokejumper Rafael Wright is there to keep her safe in Sharon Mignerey's THROUGH THE FIRE.

And now, turn the page for a sneak preview of THROUGH THE FIRE, the third installment of FAITH AT THE CROSSROADS. On sale in March 2006 from Steeple Hill Books.

Later that same afternoon Rafe met with the CSFD chief arson investigator and the two detectives assigned to the case, Samuel Vance and his partner, Becca Hilliard. Rafe had taken classes from the arson investigator, Ben Johnson, a crusty old-timer who knew more about fire than anyone Rafe had ever met. He was looking forward to seeing Ben again as much as he was dreading seeing Lucia's brother again. Since the man had come to his office and warned him to stay away from Lucia, Rafe knew he was putting her in a tough position. Since he liked her, that bothered him…it bothered him a lot.

"Glad you could make it," Ben said to Rafe as he came down the blackened hallway of the still cordoned off pediatric wing. "I sorta figured you might be out of town on one of your recruiting junkets."

"I just got back," Rafe said. "I heard on the news this was arson."

"Nobody could have been surprised about that. I'm not telling you any secrets, but nothing about this adds up. Sprinklers that don't come on, false positives on the alarm system. Time will tell if it was all coincidental or if something else was going on." Ben led the way down the hall toward the janitor's closet, or at least what was left of it.

"Personally, I never went much for coincidence."

"Finally, something we agree on," said Sam Vance, coming up behind Rafe and Ben.

"Probably more than one thing," Rafe said, his gaze moving from Sam to the woman with him.

"This is my partner, Becky Hilliard," Sam said. "Rafe Wright."

"Becca," she corrected, smiling at Rafe. "Nice to meet you. I've heard good things."

Sam shot her a glance, which made Rafe inwardly grin. "It's all true."

She laughed, turning her attention to Ben Johnson. "What's the verdict?"

Ben scratched his gray hair. "No verdict yet. I just wanted to get Rafe's take on things since he was closest to the fire and manned the extinguishers when the fire first broke out."

Rafe told the story as best he remembered it, trying to include the pertinent details of the moment when the explosion knocked him off his feet and he found Lucia on the other side of the door.

"What do you mean she was by herself?" Sam asked, latching onto the one part of the whole incident that kept bothering Rafe. "Firefighters work in teams. Where was her partner?"

"I don't know, but he wasn't with her." Rafe met

Sam's angry gaze. "I remember thinking it was a pretty strange thing at the time. And in light of O'Brien being so mad at her, the whole thing didn't make any sense. So that makes me wonder if O'Brien was somehow involved—"

"No way," Becca said. "He's a battalion fire chief responsible for the safety of his people."

"You might have a point," Sam said, "except that he's been riding Lucia ever since he was assigned to her fire station. His vendetta against her isn't new."

"Maybe not," Rafe said, "but this still makes no sense."

Ben waved to his assistant. "Track down her partner—"

"That would be Luke Donovan," Sam interrupted.

The assistant made a note in his notebook, then followed Ben down toward the blackened remains of the janitor's closet where the two of them gathered additional evidence.

"I don't know why you've taken such a personal interest in my sister," Sam said, the statement bland enough not to be a challenge. Rafe recognized it as such, however.

"Hard not to take an interest," Rafe said. "She's a special woman." He waved at the space between the two of them. "This dislike you have for me, is it your usual way of dealing with men interested in your sister, or is it more personal?"

Sam took a step toward him. "It's personal. If you can't handle that, it's real simple—you can back off."

Rafe stared at Lucia's brother, whose dark eyes were so like hers. Despite Sam's assertion his dislike was personal, Rafe had the feeling any man interested in Lucia would be equally suspect. Rafe's strong suspicion was that someone—probably a boyfriend—had badly hurt her somewhere along the way. Given her assertion that she didn't date and Sam's warning to keep his distance, that was the only thing that made sense to Rafe.

"I won't be backing off," he said to Sam. "Not until she makes it clear that's what *she* wants."

A FAMILY FOREVER

BY

BRENDA COULTER

When her fiancé was killed, pregnant Shelby Franklin's dreams were shattered. Tucker Sharpe was there to pick up the pieces and offer her a solution: marry him for the baby's sake. But would love for an unborn child be enough to keep them together?

On sale March 2006

Available at your favorite retail outlet.

www.SteepleHill.com

Steeple
Hill ®

LIAFFBC

REQUEST YOUR FREE BOOKS!

2 FREE INSPIRATIONAL NOVELS
PLUS A
FREE
MYSTERY GIFT

YES! Please send me 2 FREE Love Inspired® novels and my FREE mystery gift. After receiving them, if I don't wish to receive any more books, I can return the shipping statement marked "cancel." If I don't cancel, I will receive 4 brand-new novels every month and be billed just $3.99 per book in the U.S., or $4.74 per book in Canada, plus 25¢ shipping and handling per book and applicable taxes, if any*. That's a savings of over 20% off the cover price! I understand that accepting the 2 free books and gift places me under no obligation to buy anything. I can always return a shipment and cancel at any time. Even if I never buy another book from Steeple Hill, the two free books and gift are mine to keep forever.

113 IDN D74R   313 IDN D743

Name	(PLEASE PRINT)	
Address		Apt.
City	State/Prov.	Zip/Postal Code

Signature (if under 18, a parent or guardian must sign)

Order online at www.LoveInspiredBooks.com

Or mail to Steeple Hill Reader Service™:

IN U.S.A.	IN CANADA
3010 Walden Ave.	P.O. Box 609
P.O. Box 1867	Fort Erie, Ontario
Buffalo, NY 14240-1867	L2A 5X3

Not valid to current Love Inspired subscribers.

Want to try two free books from another series?
Call 1-800-873-8635 or visit www.morefreebooks.com

* Terms and prices subject to change without notice. NY residents add applicable sales tax. Canadian residents will be charged applicable provincial taxes and GST. This offer is limited to one order per household. All orders subject to approval. Credit or debit balances in a customer's account(s) may be offset by any other outstanding balance owed by or to the customer.

LIREG05

LESSONS FROM THE HEART

BY
DOROTHY CLARK

David Carlson's article about her fledgling literacy center uncovered long-buried memories for Erin Kelly. David's natural cynicism was rocked by Erin's courage and spirit, but overcoming the past wasn't easy. And opening David's heart to God's love might be Erin's most important lesson yet....

On sale March 2006

Available at your favorite retail outlet.

www.SteepleHill.com

Steeple Hill®

LILFH

Love Inspired
SUSPENSE

TITLES AVAILABLE NEXT MONTH

Don't miss these two stories in March

THROUGH THE FIRE by Sharon Mignerey
Faith at the Crossroads

Firefighter Lucia Vance felt the heat when she was suspended after suspicious chemicals were found at the site of a blaze she fought. With an accusation of wrongdoing hanging over her and the real culprit determined to harm her, fellow firefighter Rafael Wright's belief in her innocence was her lifeline—and possibly her only hope to survive.

WHEN SILENCE FALLS by Shirlee McCoy
Part of the LAKEVIEW miniseries

Piper Sinclair's plans to spend her summer doing research for a book were complicated when she witnessed a kidnapping, becoming a target herself. Crime scene photographer Cade Macalister knew his friend's little sister couldn't face the dangerous assailant by herself, so he was determined to protect her—whether she liked it or not.

LISCNM0206